MW00676066

SOLD AS IS

HOLLEY TRENT
author of *My Nora*

Be bold!

— Holley Trent

CRIMSON
ROMANCE
F+W Media, Inc.

This edition published by
Crimson Romance
an imprint of F+W Media, Inc.
10151 Carver Road, Suite 200
Blue Ash, Ohio 45242
www.crimsonromance.com

Copyright © 2013 by Holley Trent

ISBN 10: 1-4405-6357-8
ISBN 13: 978-1-4405-6357-7
eISBN 10: 1-4405-6358-6
eISBN 13: 978-1-4405-6358-4

This is a work of fiction. Names, characters, corporations, institutions, organizations, events, or locales in this novel are either the product of the author's imagination or, if real, used fictitiously. The resemblance of any character to actual persons (living or dead) is entirely coincidental.

Dedication

To my big sister Dee-Bo: a woman who would offer me the shirt off her back (and kindly inform me of the brand because I'm that clueless).

Hat tip to author Melissa Blue who critiqued this story while it was still in the "hot mess" stage.

Also, props to the very hip Nicole P. because . . . well, *because*.
—HT

CHAPTER 1

The sparkly pink Miata displayed on a rotating turntable on the corner of Archie's A-1 Autos' overstocked lot wasn't what made Aaron Owen stop. It did make him slow down, though. And when he slowed down, he saw the *woman*. As small as she was, she was easy to miss amongst all that steel and glass. She stood next to the turntable holding a giant price decal, and staring at the car as if it was diseased. He couldn't read the price tag, even at thirty miles per hour, and didn't really care to. The Miata wasn't what he needed. The woman, though—she was worth a closer look.

He needed five cars quick. Originally, his plan had been to pick them up at auction, but one of the things that made him so damned good at his job was his willingness to think outside the transmission box. That little saleswoman was going to cut him a deal. He could feel victory in his bones. And, yeah, while he was negotiating, he'd get a good look at the petite hustler. She *had* to be a hustler with a body like that and selling an inventory that shitty.

Aaron Owen knew shitty cars better than anyone. He'd be out of a job if he didn't.

*

Mandy McCarthy didn't know the difference between a dipstick and a decklid and gave not one iota of care to the fact. She didn't see the point of learning all that damned terminology when all she needed for minimum competence of her crappy job was to read the vehicle specs right off the inventory reports. Why else would they be taped to the drivers' side windows? Her stepfather, and owner of Archie's A-1 Autos, insisted that maybe if she did know something beyond bare minimum she'd actually sell a damned car. She wasn't so sure about that assertion because the inventory at AA1A was probably the most questionably roadworthy in all of Eastern North Carolina. Even she wouldn't buy there and she got a discount.

Not since high school had she dreaded Monday mornings so much. Back then she'd hated for weekends to end because Mondays meant horribly petrifying things such as geometry quizzes and the start of new physics units. As an adult, Mondays meant staff meetings at work followed by a lecture from her mother at home.

How old am I again?

She blew a huff of air upward to shift her too-long bangs away from her eyes and slunk lower in her seat. She thought perhaps the wall of testosterone seated in the chairs in front of hers would muddle Archie's radar for a while. She hoped it would, anyway.

"Sales are in the toilet," he barked.

She twisted her lips to one side of her face and started to chew at the inside of her mouth. Eager to avoid the man's gaze, she turned her focus up to the water stain in the drop ceiling. Archie's stare held a sort of intensity that always made her regret being born a little bit. The unblinking thing conveyed her absolute worthlessness: her *lowliness*. There were probably worms with higher self-esteem than Mandy when tasked with facing the pompous blowhard.

"It's August. We should be selling a car a day at least. People are trying to put their kids in vehicles to take to college and they come here because I'm such a nice guy," he continued.

She clamped her lips together tighter to muffle the scoff she could feel rising up in her gut. Yeah, Archie was nice, all right. He financed *everyone*. He'd also repossess on the thirty-first day after a missed payment—didn't matter if the customer only had three or four payments left. "People should pay their bills," was his party line.

He slapped the desktop and Mandy yipped.

"What are we going to do about it?"

No one said anything for a while. The only noise in the room was the sound of the overworked box air conditioning unit in the window as it hissed and whined: no match for the late-summer heat. She shifted her lips to the other side of her jaw and started to chew that side, too.

Note to self: should you ever get a job in retail management again, don't be a dick.

Archie leaned a bit sideways to see around Frank, the tow guy, and narrowed his eyes at her. She'd made the rookie mistake of looking down at exactly that moment.

Shit.

Archie pressed his lips together tightly as if he were forming the "M" in her name, but she didn't give him a chance to expel the words.

"Maybe if you listed the vehicles on the business website you'd get more people interested in coming to look at them in-person. We're kind of in the middle of nowhere, and you've got to give people some incentive to come out here. I mean, if you actually want to sell cars, that is."

His face shifted from its usual florid tones to darker pink, to red, then burgundy. He jabbed a finger in her direction and sucked in a deep breath.

"Maybe we can do a big summer sale!" her stepbrother Mike suggested with far more enthusiasm in his voice than she was certain he felt.

She felt her blood pressure began to ease down to a healthful level.

Thanks for the diversion, buddy.

Mike was her redheaded knight on the proverbial white horse, and had been since she was in ninth grade. He could never stomach her getting in trouble; even now that she was twenty-seven and he twenty-eight.

Although it was the same thing Mike suggested every week, she was off the hot seat for the moment. Archie wouldn't snap at the golden boy. Not with all the money he made him.

Mike rolled his cane back and forth over his lap. "We could call it a clearance event or something. Or maybe we can offer them some token gift with purchase. I don't know, like a license plate frame? Collegiate tee shirts or something?"

Archie shook his head and laced his fingers together atop the desk. "We just had a sale. What else you got?"

When Mike's response wasn't immediately forthcoming, Archie started rotating his big block-shaped head toward Mandy.

"Referral discounts!" Mike offered right as Mandy began to tap her foot impatiently against the floor.

She cocked her head to the side and stared at the man her mother had once told her to call "Daddy." Mandy would rather chew glass. Hell, she didn't even call her own father "Daddy," but that was another matter.

Tap-tap-tap. Her foot bounced faster against the worn carpet.

How could a man so damned ugly sire sons as handsome as Mike and Don?

She snorted and pinched herself for thinking uncharitable thoughts. Archie was married to her mother, for better or for worse. It was just that "worse" part Mandy found so goddamned offensive.

"Referral discounts?" Archie actually perked up: his lips straightening into a flat line instead of forming an upside-down U. "What's that about?"

"Uh . . . " Mike stood, being careful to bear the bulk of his weight on his good leg, and hobbled around Archie's desk to the whiteboard.

She could feel the knots in her stomach untie with every degree of rotation Archie's desk chair made counterclockwise toward the whiteboard.

Mike picked up a dry-erase marker and scribbled some frenzied calculations that actually made some sense. He was pulling out all the stops for his dad.

What the Hell is he up to?

As if he'd snatched her thoughts out of the psychic ether, Mike turned around and gave her a discreet wink before concluding, "They'll think they're getting access to exclusive inventory and lower prices . . . even if it's not true." He added that last part in a near-mumble.

The room filled with that tense quiet once more. A minute passed, then two, with no words as Archie stared at the board behind him. When he lifted his shoulders into a shrug, Mandy blew out a sigh of relief.

"Okay," he said. "Call our contact at the paper and see if we can get a sixteenth-page ad for Thursday."

Mike gave Archie a thumbs-up and limped back to his seat. While his back was still facing Archie, he rolled his eyes for Mandy's benefit. She covered her mouth and coughed to disguise the smirk that would have made Archie bark like a leashed dog that couldn't reach a squirrel.

"All right, that's it for this week," Archie said.

Maybe that fortune cookie was telling the truth last night. Today's going to be a good day!

Archie took a loud slurp of his coffee and nearly choked. "Goddamn, that's hot!" He wagged his tongue outside his mouth a few beats to cool it, and snapped his fingers at the departing staff to still them at the door. "Frank, I need you to go pick up a Camaro in Suffolk. I'll get you a check."

Frank, a scruffy bass guitarist whose recreational activities included stretching his earlobes and shotgunning tallboy cans of cheap beer, gave Archie a long blink. "Gas?"

"Same as always."

"Yeah, you keep saying that but it don't show up on my paycheck."

Archie jammed his plastic coffee stirrer straw between his teeth and chewed while giving Frank a blasé look. "Maybe you aren't reading it right. Bring in your pay stub and I'll explain it to you."

"I know how to read a pay stub. I've been reading 'em since I was fourteen."

Frank stood immediately to the right of Mandy, in perfect position for the surreptitious warning yank to his waistband. He was trying to finance his band's next tour, and wouldn't be able to manage that without income. Unfortunately, Archie was usually in a firing mood on Mondays. She'd hate for the victim of the week to be someone she actually liked.

He gave a thumb's-up behind his back as if to say, "I'm cool. Good looking out," so she let go of his belt loop.

The hinges of Archie's chair groaned as he leaned back. That damned demoralizing silence permeated the trailer once more as he rocked to and fro, staring down his pockmarked nose at Frank. Finally, in a rasp just above a whisper, he asked, "You accusing me of cheating you?"

Mandy gave one more pre-emptive yank to Frank's belt loop.

"No, I ain't saying that. I'm sayin' maybe you haven't been paying attention is all," Frank hedged.

There you go. Don't poke the rattlesnake, Frankie.

Archie jabbed the straw back between his teeth and chewed. He rocked. He stared.

Frank stared back, but couldn't sustain the intensity. He looked down at his shoes.

Mandy sighed.

"You need the address to the facility?" Archie asked.

"No. It ain't moved."

"Good. Why don't you go smoke a cigarette and I'll have a check ready by the time you get back."

Frank shifted his weight, grumbled something incomprehensible under his breath, then hauled up his pants.

Mandy stood to follow him out, and they made it as far as the door to the customer hospitality lounge when Archie called her back.

"Mandy, wait. I'm not through with you."

"Ffff-frack!" she spat in a whispered tone.

Mike, leaning against one of the Naugahyde sofas, caught her near swear and wagged his index finger at her. "You're gonna lose, girl."

She narrowed her eyes at him. "I have one more week. You haven't caught me yet and you *won't*."

The corners of his mouth turned up into the grin that made all the ladies at the track swoon. "Just a matter of time."

"Keep dreaming." She re-tucked her silk blouse, rubbed the wrinkles out of her pencil skirt, and with an artificial calm turned around in the doorway to face Archie. Solo.

Mind over matter. He's just a bully. A big, ugly bully.

She straightened her spine and put her shoulders back the way she'd been taught in poise and manners class as a child. Apparently, a lady could find courage as long as her posture was immaculate. Mandy preferred her fortification to come from Madeira or Scotch, but that was hardly appropriate before noon.

Mind over matter. He's nothing. He's just a speck of dust in the greater universe. He has no power over you.

She returned to her previous seat, crossed her legs at the ankles, and folded her hands onto her lap.

Ready as I'll ever be. "Yes, Archie?" She held her breath.

He sat upright and laced his fingers atop the desk. "I gave you this job as a favor to your mother."

She pulled her bottom lip in between her teeth and bit down into it in spite of her red lipstick. It was the only way she'd keep her tongue from wagging.

He apparently expected a retort, and when she didn't give him one, he cracked his knuckles. "All right, then. Let's not hash words.

I don't know what you did all day at the last job you had, but the fact you were there for six years says you must have actually sold something, right?"

Jackass. "Nine years, Archie. I managed a clothing store. That's a bit different than selling cars."

He guffawed. "Selling is selling. I sold animal feed. I was the best—"

"Yeah, yeah." She allowed herself the eye roll she'd been saving it up all morning. "You were the best animal feed salesman in the entire Southeast, blah blah blah."

Archie ignored her snide tone, or at least pretended to. "That's right, girlie, animal feed doesn't have a lick to do with cars but I'm a master at selling both. Know why?"

People would probably do anything to get you to go away, you evil troll. Oh, that's not nice. I'm sure trolls remember to put the toilet seat down. She managed a wry smile as she shook her head. "No, Archie, I don't know why."

"It's because I know the rules of selling. Number one is that everyone lies. The second is you should never stop at the first no. The third is—"

She put her hands up. "Okay, I get it. Sell harder."

"That's right." He pounded the desktop.

That time she didn't even jump.

"Stop trying to put yourself into everyone else's shoes, and instead, act like you know what's best for them. I believe in giving people a fair shake, but you've been here six weeks and haven't sold a thing. Even your mom has sold a car and she doesn't even work here."

"Maybe you've forgotten, but you haven't paid me anything, either. I work on commission, just like Michael, and just like Don did before he moved on to . . . "

She was going to say "greener pastures" but thought better of it. Archie wasn't worth the fight.

"Don't matter. I've got expansion plans, girlie. I need the best of the best working for me before we even think about breaking ground." He leaned forward so his eyes were level with hers.

She didn't flinch, possibly because a small part of her knew where the discussion was headed. Histrionics weren't going to make the situation easier, so she stared right back at him through her heavy bangs.

"I'm going to a base-plus-commission pay structure for my best employees. Right now you're not one of them."

"Tell me something I don't know."

He clucked his tongue as he thought and rocked side-to-side in the chair. "Okay, I'll tell you something. No!" With a snap of his fingers, he hauled himself up to his feet and walked around to the front of the desk.

She pressed her back further into the chair, but didn't look away.

"No, no, no. I'll *remind* you of something you may have forgotten. Remember what your mother said? If you're not working, you can't stay at the house. You agreed to those terms."

What choice did I have?

At the time of the agreement, she'd been hard up and two weeks from eviction. Asking her mother for help had been her last resort. She'd been denied unemployment benefits, had drained her meager savings, and for once, Mike didn't have cash to loan her. He was going through his own shit. Bad luck all around.

She'd actually been floored after laying it all bare only for her mother to respond to her with a noncommittal "I'll have to call you back." And she did—the next night, with Archie's restrictions.

He snapped his fingers in front of her face to jostle her back to attention. "You've got two weeks. You need to sell one-half of what Mike averages or you gotta go."

She stared at him without response for a moment while his words settled in. He was asking her to go from zero to sixty in one second flat. Scalding heat spread up from her pounding heart to her cheeks, rendering her a bit lightheaded. She was seeing stars, but didn't know if they were from rage or the effects of her circulation. Without too much twitching, she forced her lips into her patented *eat shit* grin. "I understand, Archie."

He didn't look like he believed it, but didn't call her on her lack of sincerity. "Well, get to work, then."

"Yes. I'll do that," she said through clenched teeth.

"'Preciate your cooperation. Send Frank in."

"Sure thing." She took her time clearing out of the office. She uncrossed her legs slowly. Worked some imaginary wrinkles out of her dark skirt. Checked that her shirt was tucked in all around. And with a mere bob of her head toward Archie as acknowledgement, she stood and walked to the lounge with the all the speed of a turtle in stilettos.

Once she'd cleared the threshold and was standing near the refreshment center—a mini fridge stocked with store-brand sodas and a shelf of stale cracker packs—she turned her arms around in their sockets like the blades of a windmill and did a silent scream that did nothing to diminish her desire to spew an articulate stream of profanity. "Grr!"

Now even more enraged, she stomped across the worn carpet, threw open the storm door, and nearly tossed herself down the trailer's concrete stairs into her stepbrother's arms when the heel of her pump got caught on the aluminum threshold.

Mike grabbed her by the shoulders right before her face smacked the ground.

"Shit!" Now that she was safely upright, he stooped to rub his busted knee.

She felt a surge of guilt for aggravating the thing. That knee was why he was working at that dump in the first place.

He blew out a shuddering breath as he massaged his leg and asked, "What happened?" without looking up.

She leaned over, put her hands on her knees, and concentrated on her own breathing. That fall had scared the shit out of her. What if that had been a customer? They would have sued Archie for everything including the shirt off his back. If she said anything, Archie would say, "Well, go get a hammer and fix it. Are you that dumb?"

She found her breath. "Archduke Ass-uh . . . *astronaut* says if I don't meet his arbitrary sales quota within two weeks I'm toast."

Mike grunted as he picked up his cane and forced himself erect. "Damn. Almost had you there. So, what's the quota?"

"I have to sell half as many cars in two weeks as you do."

"Great. Normally, I'd say it'd be a breeze for you to do half of the zero I feel like selling in the next two weeks, but I need cash. Don't worry. We'll figure something out."

She sighed. "You're sweet, Mike, but don't worry about me. You've done enough for me the past couple of months, and I think I'm all out of favors. I'll figure something out."

He narrowed intelligent green eyes at her and crossed his arms over his pinstriped dress shirt. When he spoke again his voice held a tinge of doubt. "Like what, Mandy? You've been applying to clothing stores for management jobs for three months and not a single one of them has extended an offer."

"Yeah, well." She raked her fingers through her long bob and pulled her hair with a cavewoman grunt. "It's the goddaaaaa-uh . . . dang! The *dang* references. They all want to know why I left Ermine's, and I guess the story doesn't work for them."

"God," he whispered, carefully unclenching her fingers from her locks and holding her shaking hands in his. "Mandy, it's okay. You're all right. We'll figure something out, okay?" He smiled that smile that made everything seem honky-dory, even when it wasn't.

She grinned and let out the breath she'd been holding.

"Let's get these cars unlocked. I'll get the keys from the safe."

"Yeah. Okay." With a sigh, she put up her hands and took

steps toward the back lot. "Business as usual. Just let me get some sunscreen out of my glove compartment. Probably best for me to stay out of the trailer today."

"I agree," he said to her retreating back.

"Oh, Mike, by the way," she called out, turning her head just before rounding the corner, but still walking. "Can you get my—"

She didn't get the words out, because she plowed front-first into a tall, dark, and handsome column of a man originating from the other direction.

CHAPTER 2

"I'm sorry," the dark-haired baritone said. He cringed to reveal perfectly straight white teeth and bent down with a hand extended to aid her up.

Mandy rubbed her sore neck and gawked up at him from the ground her ass had smacked after he'd bumped her. She knew that face.

"I was just looking for some help." He hooked his thumb in the direction of the back lot when she didn't take his hand. "I parked back there and was talking to your tow guy for a few minutes while he smoked. He told me to come back up to the trailer to get some sales help since your meeting was over. Please let me help you up. I don't usually go around knocking pretty girls on their rears."

His voice was like molten lava: thick, deep and bearing a hint of a drawl that marked him a true native. *Lord have mercy, he could read the McDonald's dollar menu and sound like hot, dirty sex.* She cleared her throat and blinked at him. God forbid he say anything scandalous or else she would probably melt into a little puddle there at his feet, just like all the other girls did. That was the problem: she didn't want to be like all the other girls. Begging for crumbs of attention at a man's feet had never been her style, and she wasn't going to start then. Not even for *that* man, prize that he was.

She put her hand in his when he offered it once more and allowed him to pull her gracefully up to her feet.

"There you go." He smiled and let his rough hand linger around hers, and she allowed it because she'd experienced a mental disconnect between what she'd expect and what reality turned out to be.

The hands she figured would be soft and manicured were tipped with dirty fingernails and had calluses on the palms. Oh

17

no, this wasn't a man who spent entire days behind a desk. This was a man who created things. A man who didn't just oversee a chore, but who actually engaged in it himself. A doer. A rebel?

Holy Hell.

Her head reeled. Everything she thought she knew about the governor's son suddenly seemed questionable.

She finally let go of his hand and took a few steps back, swiping dirt off her rear in the process. Somehow, she found her voice, although it came out sounding thick and choked. "Mr. Owen, what are you doing in Edenton?"

He didn't answer right away, and it didn't take her long to figure out why. Even though shielded the mirrored lenses of his aviator sunglasses, it was obvious where his gaze was fixed.

Great. Another letch.

She looked down to ensure her headlights hadn't been turned on, and instead discovered she'd lost a button sometime between their collision and the morning meeting.

Damn it.

She pulled the plackets of her shirt together at the neck and crossed her arms over her chest. The button must have bounced when she was flailing her arms around like a whirligig in the hospitality lounge.

He grinned and she wanted to smack it off his gorgeous face. "I was in the area . . . "

Suddenly, Mike opened the storm door and hobbled down the stairs with the keys, whistling a jaunty little tune while he moved. His gaze flitted to her, and she shifted her weight nervously. She'd had a change of heart. Suddenly, being in the office with Archie seemed a lot less humiliating than bumbling repeatedly in front of the Adonis.

"Well, I'll be." Mike had his hand extended to shake Aaron's before he even reached the bottom stair. "Mike Leonard. I'm the son of the guy who owns this dump."

She thought her stomach was going to jump up through her throat and choke her to death. Mike was probably the most charming guy she knew, although his tactics sometimes frightened her. He managed to sell cars with leaking ceilings, missing carpet, and a host of other problems because he shot straight from the hip and never sold a family more than they could afford. If that meant a near-jalopy? Fine. As long as it passed state inspection.

Archie wasn't so discriminating. In his opinion, pretty was more important than functional. The cars were labeled 'Sold As Is' so whenever folks complained, he just threw his hands up and reminded them with a sneer: "Caveat emptor. You bought it, you keep it. Unless you stop paying for it, that is."

"Oh, I wouldn't say *dump*." Aaron pushed his sunglasses to the top of his head to reveal kind hazel eyes that wrinkled at the edges when he smiled.

Oh, sweet fuck, he looks better in person.

She ripped her gaze away and started to chew at the inside of her cheeks again as she pretended to study the nearby row of cars.

"My charity expanded into this area six months ago. We've got a huge backlog of applicants I'm trying to assist before the end of the year. Got some grant money to use up."

"Didn't want to check out the auctions?" Mike asked.

"Usually do, but this is time-sensitive. I've got folks in the queue with jobs they can't get to, and they all live in this county."

Mike shifted his cane to his other hand and scoffed. "So you're gonna pay retail for convenience? Come on, man."

Aaron raised a hand to chest level and splayed his fingers. "Five cars. I think you could afford to cut me some slack. I'm not looking for high-end. I'll gladly drive a couple cars off the lot that need some love as long as they're mechanically sound."

Mike whistled low and gave Mandy's ribs an indiscreet bump with his elbow. "Five cars, huh?"

She rubbed her side and gave him a glower she hoped didn't require translation.

He was undeterred. "You do all the buying, Mr. Owen?"

"Not anymore. When I first started Cars to Work I handled it all, but really, I'm a gear head at heart. I'd rather be fixing cars than burnin' up the roads trying to cut deals. My procurement workers do the bulk of the shopping now." Aaron shifted his gaze away from Mike and cranked up the wattage on that crooked smile for Mandy's benefit.

She didn't return it. So maybe he wasn't as clean cut as she previously believed, but she knew his type. Playboy lothario so hung up on himself he thought the moon shone at night as a tribute to him. He was gorgeous. She'd give him that. However, gorgeous had never been enough for her. She needed substance, and that was why she tended to date guys like Frank who had quirks and dysfunctions, even if they weren't pretty.

He turned back to Mike. "Now that the organization has enough workers to cover almost every county, I don't have to be everywhere at once. My team is strong and I'm trying to grow it so we can get more done."

"Oh yeah? Why do I get the feeling we're not talking about buying or selling cars?" Mike asked.

Mandy hadn't gotten that feeling at all, but Aaron shrugged. "You're right. I've become pretty brazen about headhunting people to work for CTW. I steal people who know cars. The auto part stores don't like me very much nowadays."

Mike and Mandy shared a look.

Aaron pushed his sunglasses back onto his nose and shoved his hands into the pockets of his cargo shorts. "Anyhow, first things first. We can discuss my corporate structure in detail later if you're so inclined, but I need to buy cars right now. What can you show me that doesn't already have one tire in the grave?"

*

Aaron tried to stay out of the way while the staff of A-1 Autos worked themselves up into a froth. He'd hoped just once for a quiet transaction, but the moment Archie had come to the door to chastise Mike and Mandy for standing around, things turned frantic. Suddenly half the staff materialized from out of the blue to unlock car doors and prop up hoods.

"Mandy! Don't just stand there in the way. That pick-up that came in yesterday needs its wheels cleaned. Get on it. Michael! Get the man a drink. Would you like something to drink, Mr. Owen?"

Aaron watched the terse brunette turn on her heel and click-clack away toward the back lot, mumbling under her breath as she retreated.

Little hellcat.

He chuckled. What she was lacking in size, she made for in curves: pert breasts, narrow waist, and a round bottom that strained against the back of her pencil skirt. In the back of his mind, he had a slight awareness of Archie on the trailer steps running his mouth, but the voice was like a gnat buzzing in is ear. Inconsequential. Hardly important. Now, the sound of Mandy's clicking heels against the asphalt and the movement of her ass when she walked? Those rated attention.

When she finally rounded the corner, he tuned back in to the theatrics orchestrated by Archie. The lot owner was looking right at him, waiting for a response.

Shit. What did he ask? Aaron slipped a hand into a pocket of his shorts and wrapped his fingers around the ink pen inside, squeezing it as he sorted his thoughts. *Oh, yeah. A drink.*

"No, thank you for asking, though. I'm actually in a bit of a hurry. Got a staff meeting in Durham at two, so if it's all right with you, I'll just take a look around and see if there's anything that pops out at me." Other than Mandy, he meant.

"Sure, sure! Why don't you let my Mike show you around? He knows everything about everything. He wouldn't steer you wrong."

Aaron couldn't be completely sure, but he thought he caught a glimpse of Mike rolling his eyes behind his father's back. Aaron studied the ginger's face for a moment, waiting for him to meet his eyes, and when he did his beyond the slight twitching of his jaw hinges, his expression was blank.

What the Hell kind of family business is this?

"So, how 'bout it?" Archie pressed.

Aaron pushed his suspicions aside for the moment. He was probably just being overly paranoid as usual. He couldn't help it, growing up the way he had.

"Yeah," he agreed. "Fine."

As Archie returned to his inner sanctum to do whatever Archie did, Mike limped over and grabbed Aaron by the elbow with his free hand. "Come on," he said, nudging him in the opposite direction from Archie's open window. Once sufficiently out of Archie's auditory range, Mike blew out a breath and rubbed his eyes.

"Look, let me be candid. There are only two or three cars here I'm confident enough in to sell to you. The rest are jalopies, junkers, or have weird smells. Some are barely roadworthy. We have a guy on staff that keeps them running well enough to get off the lot, but beyond that . . . " He lifted his shoulders in a shrug.

"Hmm." Aaron leaned against the trailer wall and twirled his pen between his fingers. That mechanic sounded like someone he needed to meet. He'd been recruiting guys and girls away from thirty-dollar oil change shops, and they'd been hit or miss for what he needed. Mostly miss. CTW's lead mechanic Eleanor had been his greatest coup, and boy did her daddy hate him for snatching her out of their shop. He still got threatening phone calls from the guy weekly.

Mike bent at the waist and massaged his right knee. "They're going to take me out back and shoot me at the rate I'm falling apart."

Aaron chuckled. Mike wasn't the fox in the skirt he'd made a U-turn to transact with, but he seemed like a nice guy. He'd hire him in a New York minute, if only for the secretaries back in CTW's Durham headquarters. They were running short on eye-candy. At least, that's what they told him every time he dropped by the office to pick up files or check messages. "Aaron, I know you want folks who can put engines together with their eyes closed, but could you at least hire one who'd be nice to wake up next to? Just one?" his secretary Jasmine had whined. He hadn't known how to respond. He'd merely scratched his head and left.

"Good to know about the cars upfront," he said, watching Mike grip the handle of his cane with a renewed cringe as he stood. "But why are you telling me? Seems like a conflict of interest."

Mike shrugged. "I give everyone who steps foot onto this lot the same lecture. I abide by the 'do unto others' rule 'cause I need to be able to sleep at night. So, there you go—the Mikey L. guarantee." He held up his hand in a scout's honor gesture. "If you want someone who really shoots from the hip, though, talk to Mandy. She's not going to try to sell you anything."

Aaron shook his head, not understanding his point. "And that's good, how?"

Mike grinned. "You know cars."

"Yeah, I do."

"And she doesn't."

"Ah."

Honest and knowledgeable. I wonder how much he'd expect me to pay him.

He reached into his pocket for his wallet, intending to hand Mike his business card, but before he could sort through the pile of unsorted receipts he'd stuffed into the thing, Mandy hobbled past. She was struggling with a bucket full of sudsy water and clamping a scrub brush between her white teeth. He could just barely make out the not-quite-swear words she was mumbling under her breath. They were vicious enough she might as well had gone all the way. He looked to Mike for explanation.

Mike laughed and shook his head. "She's got a bad habit of using curse words to replace most nouns, adjectives, and adverbs in a sentence. I made a bet with her last week she couldn't go without cursing for two weeks."

"Ah. I would have lost that bet on the first day. Well, what do you get if she slips up?"

Mike hooked his thumbs into the pockets of his slacks and smiled broadly. "She has to go to Hooters with me."

"For the wings, right? Isn't that the lie everyone tells?"

Mike shook his head. "Nope. I'd make her go just to see her blush."

A woman with a mouth like that was capable of blushing? Aaron couldn't believe it. Must have been some backstory missing.

"She worked there for about six months in college until she found a gig that didn't require wearing short-shorts."

"Ah. Well, what does she get if you don't catch her?"

"She couldn't come up with anything. I think deep down inside she knows she's going to lose this one. She's got a mouth like a Scottish pirate, and probably the temper of one, too."

"Jesus."

They both watched as water from the overfilled pail sloshed onto her navy polka-dotted pumps. She paused to pull her shoes off by the heels, and Aaron fixed his stare onto her tanned thighs as her skirt rode up in the back.

I wonder if it's natural or a fake bake like Elly gets.

Real or not, his little sister didn't have thighs like that. Elly was a waif. Mandy had the kind of thighs he'd seen on women who rode horses, and the longer he stared, the longer he wondered if maybe she *did* like to ride. He blew out a breath and jammed his pen back into his pocket.

"Yeah, after fifteen years I've gotten used to it."

"Mm hmm." *What were we talking about? Cars or something? Get it together, man.*

She was making it damned hard for him. As she pulled of her second heel, the slit in her skirt rode up to where her underwear should have started. Aaron tuned Mike out once more as she crouched, his gaze fixed on her legs until the fabric stopped shifting.

Nope. No dice, no view.

He snapped out of the siren's trance and rushed over to aid her. After all, he was raised to be a Southern gentleman, not some ogling pervert.

"Here, why don't you let me carry that bucket?" Anticipating her consent, he wrapped his hand around the handle right next to hers.

"No thanks!" She gave the handle an abrupt yank, which made the contents splash up onto the silk blouse he'd earlier admired. The moisture adhered the delicate fabric to her chest and made the outline of her demi-bra prominent.

She was all Mandy, no padding.

"Shit."

"Yeah, you said it, guy." She closed her eyes and took several deep breaths. Once her shoulders stopped twitching, she unwrapped her fingers from the bucket handle and slowly straightened to her full five feet tall.

If it weren't for the filter provided by the fringe of dark bangs over her gray eyes, the intensity of her stare might have rendered him dumb. He suddenly understood what Mike meant about that temper.

"Crap, I'll get you something to dry off with," Mike said as he hobbled to the trailer. "I've got a tee shirt in my car if you want it."

Her voice was low and flat when she responded. "I'll pass. It's thin. It'll dry."

Now alone with the ticking time bomb, Aaron wasn't sure how to react. Try to defuse her with his charm? That worked on most women he engaged with, but somehow he didn't think a smile and wink would work on this one. She needed extra finessing, and he didn't mind so much, because even with the sneer and knitted eyebrows, she was the most beautiful woman he'd ever seen.

She was interesting. Unusual, even. Something other than the typical English rose type his father had always been so fond of and which his mother fit squarely into. And, the longer he stared, the more intoxicating she seemed.

Holy Hell, those eyes.

But it wasn't the gray gaze burning holes through him he found most striking. That prize went to her skin. She had a flawless olive complexion that made her look a bit like a highly polished statue come to life. The hair was nice, too—a long chestnut bob that took on a bronzy tone in the morning sun. He didn't know much about clothes, but her style was evident. Modern without being excessively trendy. Classic, even. She was like an Audrey Hepburn for a new millennium, but one with more oomph to sink his teeth into.

No, this wasn't a time to be smarmy. She wasn't a reporter to feed some pre-scripted line to. She wasn't one of the women trying to snag him with the goal of to marrying up. Hell, she looked like she couldn't give a shit about him. Boy, did that flip his switch in the right direction.

"I'm sorry," he said, hoping the simple statement was the right one. Every muscle in his body seemed to coil as he endured her continued scrutiny.

Finally, the tight set of her jaw eased, and her shoulders inched away from her ears. Crisis averted.

He exhaled his relief.

She flicked at her shirt. "I can't seem to keep these blouses clean. I got hot dog chili on the last one I wore to work."

Aaron felt the contents of his stomach begin to roil and struggled to swallow. "Hot dog chili?" he rasped.

"Yeah. Classy." She accepted the wad of paper towels Mike returned with and started patting her shirt dry.

Aaron turned to Mike for elaboration.

"Sometimes Dad does these used car carnivals," he said. "Lame-ass games, cheap food, and a lot of helium-filled latex balloons. People seem to dig them. Customers like to think they're getting something extra with their car purchase, even if they'll digest the 'extra' in four hours."

Archie knocked on the side window and made a "What are you doing?" gesture at the trio.

Michael grinned wide and gave the man a thumb's-up. "Everything's great!" he said, putting overly exaggerated emphasis on his words so Archie could read his lips. Archie rolled his eyes and backed away. Aaron turned his attention back to the doused vixen.

"Look, Mandy, I really am sorry about your shirt. Will you let me get it dry-cleaned for you? Or, I don't know. How does one clean silk?"

She scoffed and finally let a smile crack her face. "Honestly? I usually just take them off when I get home, sniff 'em, and if they're not too offensive I hang 'em up until the next time. If they need some attention, I hand wash. I don't give dry cleaners my hard-earned money." Her small grin wilted just that quickly.

What's that about? Dry cleaning is an odd thing to be sensitive over.

She resumed the dabbing of her shirt and he resumed staring at the way her nipples strained behind it as she blotted.

It took Mike holding out another dry length of paper towels for Aaron to pull his gaze away. He couldn't remember a single time when he'd been so instantly aroused by a woman. Between that husky voice of hers and the *fuck-off* attitude, he was whipped. Absolutely ensnared.

Mike to the rescue again. "Hey, Mandy, my knee is killing me." He bent down and picked up the bucket's handle. "If I stay upright much longer I'm going to be crawling by lunchtime."

She was still attending her soiled shirt so she didn't see the *I got this* wink Mike gave Aaron.

"Why don't you let me worry about the dirty wheel spokes, huh? I'll get myself a crate to sit on and you can show Mr. Owen the three sedans with the premium stickers? Can you do me that favor?"

She performed a graceful hair flip that cleared her bangs from her eyes and revealed her arched eyebrow. The smell of vanilla wafted to Aaron's nose and without realizing it until too late, he took a step closer to her.

"I don't know anything about those cars. They haven't been here long enough," she said.

Mike sputtered his lips and squeezed the bridge of his nose between his thumb and forefinger. "I'm sorry, Mr. Owen. Can you excuse us for a moment?"

Aaron retrieved his pen from his pocket and twirled it yet again as he pondered Mike's exasperation. "Sure," he said finally. "I'll just start looking at that blue one. Are the doors open?"

"Yes," Mike and Mandy said in unison.

Aaron nodded and walked toward the row of newer vehicles. When he looked behind him, Mike was making wild gestures and Mandy was shaking her head.

Aaron leaned against the side of the open sedan and tapped his pen on top of the doorframe. "What an odd little sales team," he mumbled. "Why are they working here? They're both out of place."

He woke up his phone and told it to call his number four speed dial contact. When Tina answered with a "What do you need, dude?" in lieu of "hello" he said, "Honey, I need you to do some pre-employment screening on a few folks. I don't have a whole lot of info, but hold tight for a bunch of text messages. Be discreet, as always."

He listened to Tina chatter in her usual rocket-propelled cadence, then chuckled. "I guess he's okay looking. Not really my type."

He walked around to the front of the car and stared at the engine without touching. It was clean as a whistle, which meant absolutely nothing. Clean didn't mean functional. Besides, that engine had way too little power for a car that size. He hated base models.

"So, how's this going to affect the training event?" Tina asked.

"I don't know if it is." He worked his way to the driver's door and sank into the seat. "Still, can't hurt to be prepared. We can add another room. Better to have it than not."

"You know, I don't mind handling some logistical stuff every now and then, but this really isn't—"

"Objection noted, Tina." He pushed his sunglasses up to the top of his hair and rested his forehead on the steering wheel. "I know it's not your job. I'm working on finding someone who can do it. You know how picky I am, especially since that last batch of dud mechanics. I won't compromise my core team with warm bodies who won't pull their weight. I'll make it right for both you and Chas. Just give me some time."

"Fine." Tina sighed and hung up.

CHAPTER 3

"Come on, Mike, I know you're trying to help me out, but this could be a big deal for you. You said you needed cash, right? Maybe you could finally get that knee of yours fixed."

Mandy and Mike both turned their gazes toward Aaron. He was talking on his phone and had his back turned to them while he stared under the hood of one of the sedans.

Mike slid his arm around her shoulder and moved them a bit further from Archie's office window. "Don't worry about my knee," he whispered. "I'll be insured soon enough. I didn't want to say anything yet because Dad's gonna blow his top, but I've got another gig lined up."

She ducked out from under his arm and put her hands on her hips, scowling at him. "I never tell your secrets."

He nodded. "I know that. I just—" He blew out a breath and shifted his weight to his good side. "I didn't want you to feel like you were being left dangling. It's a good gig. Evening news doing sports commentary. The station had offered me the position way back when I was still competing, but I wasn't ready to sit still."

"And now you don't have a choice." She pointed to his bum knee.

He shrugged. "Look, I'm just trying to hold out until payday because Dad is bastard enough he would hang onto my final commission check if I quit. I just need to make it look like I'm trying. I'll sell that Miata or something, so you go ahead and take the Owen commission."

She pushed her hair back from her eyes and furrowed her brow. "You ginger jerk. I can't believe you."

He smiled in that smarmy way he reserved especially for her.

She rolled her eyes.

"I haven't told anyone else. I wanted to make sure it was a done deal before I started making announcements. I faxed the paperwork from Dad's office before he came in this morning. I hope he doesn't check the history."

"You're a horrible son!" Even as she said it she started to giggle and wrapped an arm around his waist to lean her head on his shoulder.

"That I am."

They both laughed. Truth was, they'd been in a tacit conspiracy to make "Archduke Asshole's" life as uncomfortable as they could manage for the past fifteen years. Usually, Mandy didn't need to try all that hard. She just had to be herself and sit back and wait for the tirades about her uselessness. Mike had to work a little harder. His last great stunt had been nearly breaking his back after being tossed from his motorcycle during a motocross event in Sanford. He broke his shin in two places and the ligaments of his right knee were all over the place. Since he hadn't been back on the track in almost a year, his endorsements dried up, followed immediately by his savings. Him nearly killing himself hadn't been what flustered Archie: Mike having to move in with him did *that*.

"I totally am. I think I'm his cosmic payback for all the dirt he's done in life. I don't know how your mom puts up with him. Hell, I don't know how *my* mom put up with him for ten years. I never knew she was capable of laughing until after the divorce was final. That's how much it sucked."

"I hate you for leaving me to the wolves." She shifted her lips to the right side of her face and started chewing the inside of her mouth again. Mike being at the house was the only pro to balance out a very long list of cons in respect to her moving back home with her tail between her legs. He just *got* her. She didn't have to explain anything.

Mike held her close and rested the side of his face on top of her head. "Aw, kid. I know it's rough. Just keep asking around, flexin' that network of yours. You'll find a job soon. I just know it. Meanwhile, go sell that man those cars. It's an easy sale. Just be honest and sit back and collect your free money."

"Easy for you to say. I get hung up on even the simplest questions." She pulled away from his arm so she could up into his face. "What is the difference between a diesel engine and a gasoline one, anyway?"

He opened his mouth, closed it, and then flattened his lips into a straight line. After thirty seconds or so, he finally offered, "Hey, that might require a diagram. Just keep on tellin' folks that diesel is more efficient for long-distance hauling, okay?"

She shook her head. "I'm not going to remember that. I can walk through four rows of a clothing store and point out every display that's not to spec or schedule a staff of sixty people for a week of irregular shifts, but don't expect me to remember what a bunch of moving parts do and why."

"Don't beat yourself up over it. We can't all be good at everything."

"Truer words were never spoken." Aaron approached the two with a clipboard in his large hands and turned the full bore of his movie star grin on Mandy.

She gulped but straightened her posture and stuck out her chin.

"I actually suck at a lot of things. Makes life easier to just fess up to it and hire someone who's good at those things to do them for me."

"Amen," Mike agreed. "Did you see anything you like, Mr. Owen?"

Aaron looked down at his clipboard and clucked his tongue as he reviewed some notes. "I want to try to lock down that green sedan today. It's a really desirable car for people with small children because of the deep and wide backseat. We have a Tyner family on our waitlist with twin infants and a toddler who would need to put three car seats in the back. If it runs well, I'll take it off your hands today. There are a couple of others that might be okay, but I'll have to come back for those."

"Cool. Well, Mandy will take care of you. If you have any questions—"

"I won't be able to answer them," she rebutted. Mike had said to be honest, so she would.

Aaron's grin wilted a bit, not into a frown, but into something less salacious—more *encouraging*. "That's all right. I'm an engineer and a car enthusiast. I can identify the source of pretty much any ticking or clattering just from hearing it. If the ride isn't smooth, it's not hard for me to figure out why. All I need from you is general information about where the car came from and stuff like that."

He was twirling that pen again, but doing it slowly enough that Mandy could see the dirt under his nails. Yeah, she was intrigued, and becoming more so with each passing minute with him on the lot. In every picture she'd seen him in on television or in newspapers, he'd been well groomed and immaculately dressed. Even when he was just out on short errands his appearance seemed carefully curated: crisp polo shirts and khakis, hair slicked back, and those mirrored sunglasses always perched on his nose. The man in the pictures looked like the sort who would be averse to fiddling around under a sooty car hood.

Standing in front of her was a different person altogether. His sun-streaked brown hair was longish—not long enough to require a ponytail, but certainly long enough to need frequent tucking behind his ears since he hadn't styled it that day. His blue ringer tee had a hole at the neck he had to have been aware of and his tan shorts had a couple of bleach splotches. She thought this version of Aaron Owen, with the five o'clock shadow on his chiseled face and wearing an easy, affable smile, was far more interesting than his public persona. This casual Aaron was the kind of guy she would gleefully seduce. His alter ego was the kind of guy she could corrupt. She always felt bad for being corruptive.

Mike gave her a nudge with his elbow. "Why are smiling like that, Miranda? Did you lose your last marble?"

"Possibly. It was lonely. It was bound to roll away sooner or later."

She didn't know if Aaron was reading her mind or if they were just on the same wavelength. His smile had changed yet again. It had gone from being merely pleasant to a bit crooked, flirtatious.

Mike obviously didn't notice. "Don't worry, Mr. Owen. She's quite competent, even if she is a bit insane."

"Well, good. I could use the entertainment. I've been out at the beach alone on prescribed R&R time by my mother for the past week and was bored out of my skull. So, test drive?"

"Of course. I'll go get the key. I guess we can forego copying your license. You're not exactly a nobody."

"According to my mother anyway." Aaron kept his gaze locked on her face until the door slammed behind Mike. Together, they started walking toward the sedan. "So, how did a stunner like you end up in a place like this?"

Her brows shot up but she fixed her face before he looked down at her again. "I bet you say that to all the girls, Mr. Owen."

"Aaron. Call me Aaron."

"Fine. Aaron."

"So, tell me."

They stopped at the car trunk and waited for Mike to catch up. "It's a long story and not particularly flattering."

"You mean selling cars isn't your first choice profession?"

She laughed a hearty, gut-clenching laugh and could hardly catch her breath. "No way. This wasn't even a plan B. I double-majored in business administration and human resources. I thought that degree would keep me away from this place."

"Wow."

"Wow what?"

He opened his mouth, but closed it without saying anything. Instead, he shook his head and held out an arm, indicating she continue toward the car.

"Anyhow, I had a great job I loved back in Raleigh. I got fired three months ago."

"Over anything scandalous?"

She shook her head as Mike hobbled over holding out the key. She took it and waved him away. "Nothing that makes a good story. Just corporate bullsh-uh . . . crap."

"Damn it!" Mike exclaimed from up the lot.

They got into the car with Aaron in the driver's seat and her at his right.

"I've never really had a job to be fired from," he admitted as he turned the ignition.

"How'd you manage that?"

He shrugged. "Rich parents. Or at least they were rich by the time I had any awareness of such things. I went straight from college to a service program. Dug ditches and built shelters in third world countries—that kind of thing. Did that for five years then moved home right when Dad was campaigning for governor."

"Let's head south on 32."

He nodded and carefully backed the car out of its diagonal space into the driveway. "I wasn't home for long when I started the Cars to Work charity. Actually, my mother urged me to do it. I was getting nagged so much by the national press because they couldn't figure out what I was about."

She remembered the press's interest in him. At the time, it hadn't been because he'd done anything spectacular, but more so because he gorgeous and mysterious, and his father was being touted as a future presidential candidate for the party. No one knew anything about what made the man tick, and he always played coy with the press, leaving folks to think what they would. Just like Mandy had.

"Still can't, I guess."

"Right. Well, it was either I do something productive or take one of those offers to sign onto the cast of a reality television show. The charity seemed like the more fruitful endeavor."

"I tend to agree."

"Other folks did, too. Money started pouring in."

She turned in her seat so her knees were angled toward him and her back to the passenger door. "You've never worked for anyone other than charities, although you could probably land a pretty sweet job in any number of corporations due to your father's connections—"

"And?"

"And instead, here you are running the fastest growing NPO in the state. Do you even pay yourself?"

He snorted and stole a look at her as he braked for a stoplight. At that angle his eyes looked straight green, although back at the lot there'd been a smattering of brown in them. "Yes, I pay myself, although my admin's paychecks look a little better than mine. It's been a wild ride, but it hasn't been easy."

"Explain."

"I've got a staff of around thirty scattered all over the state and parts of Virginia. Caseworkers, certified mechanics, project managers, administrative and marketing folks, and so on. Everyone does their own thing and once a quarter or so my mother sends me some guy who makes sure I have all the board meetings on time and that I get all my paperwork in."

"I'm not hearing a problem yet." As the light switched to green, she pointed right.

"The problem is I never know where anyone is at any given time. I don't want to be at my computer poring over schedules. I want to be out in the field talking to the people we help and, well, playing with cars."

"You should hire someone."

He cast his green gaze in her direction. "I'm working on it. So, hey, can we take this car out to open road? I want to put some stress on the engine."

"You got it. Swing a U and we'll go barrel down Highway 17."

This was the kind of test drive she could get used to. He didn't ask her complicated questions like when he should shift into all wheel drive or why there wasn't an external antenna. He already knew.

And maybe it didn't hurt he was gorgeous. If she had to put her car-related idiocy on display, it might as well be for someone she could daydream about later.

CHAPTER 4

"So, Miranda, is it?" Aaron pushed the accelerator nearly to the floorboard after checking the mirrors for signs of Chowan County's finest. "Isn't Mandy traditionally short for Amanda?"

He was curious indeed about her nickname, but not just for personal reasons.

"Normally it is." She leaned closer to the center console and turned off the country music station that had been programmed into the pre-sets by someone at the lot. "Mike started calling me Mandy right around the time our parents hooked up. It started as Mirandy as a tease. He used to sing it and dance around like it was a taunt, knowing he was pushing my buttons. It sort of morphed from there. Everyone in Chowan County calls me Mandy now."

"Which do you prefer? Mandy or Miranda?"

She straightened up in her seat and turned her head to watch the forest as they raced past. "Slow down at that curve up there. It's a speed trap."

He nodded and let off the pedal. Sure enough, hidden 10 meters down a wooded path was a highway patrol vehicle. He probably could have gotten out of any ticket, but he didn't want her to know that. Besides, he didn't like flexing those diplomatic muscles. It was nice to know they were there if he needed them, but he preferred not to advantage of political perks. He hadn't earned them, after all. His father had.

"I suppose it depends on who's saying my name. Whenever Archie calls me Mandy I want to correct him, but I suspect that's just me being contrary."

"And are you contrary? By nature, I mean?"

She smiled. "Yeah. Unfortunately, I am. It's one of my few major faults."

He laughed at the flatness of her voice while saying that.

Oh, she's cute.

"What are your other major faults?"

Be a little less obvious, will ya, guy? If you're gonna do a job interview, how about you ask some questions you haven't read off a list before?

Superficially, Mandy seemed ideal for the job he had in mind. Between her education and her take-no-shit attitude, she'd fit in great with the CTW hooligans. But what he couldn't decide was whether hiring her would be trouble. And, yeah, she looked a lot like trouble and sounded like it, too, with the way his cock constricted every time one of those throaty laughs escaped her throat.

"I'm not sure if I can discuss those with a stranger," she said finally.

"Oh, I see. Well, we don't have to be strangers."

"What exactly would the getting-to-know-you process entail? Hmm? I know your type, Mr. Owen. I bet you have a girlfriend in every podunk town in the state."

"Call me Aaron, remember? And that's just ridiculous. Let's not play fishing games, sweetheart. If you want to know if I have a girlfriend, just ask." Hell, he wanted her to ask. That way he could turn the table. A girl like that had to have someone she went home to. If not, something was wrong with the men in Edenton.

She crossed her arms over those fabulous breasts and shrugged under her seatbelt. "I don't care if you have a girlfriend."

"Oh, that burns!" He smiled and stole another look. Her jaw was tight and face otherwise devoid of expression. He must have pushed a button. Still, he figured one more little nudge couldn't hurt. "Really? You have no interest whatsoever in the life of a pseudo celebrity?"

She rooted through her purse and pulled out black-framed sunglasses that reminded him of a pair his mother owned. Mom had gotten them from Ermine's before Ermine's started going downhill. She'd been complaining for two months that the manager was a useless snot.

The more he stared at Mandy, the more the purse seemed familiar, too.

Must be spending too much time around Elly if I'm starting to recognize handbags.

Instead of putting the sunglasses on the bridge of her nose, Mandy pushed them past her temples like a headband to hold her bangs back from her eyes. He appreciated the unimpeded view so he could better study her features. She had a high forehead and a bit of a widow's peak that made her seem even more glamorous.

"I may not be interested in you specifically, but I am interested in your charity. I think it's a good cause—getting cars to poor rural folks so they can get to work. I believe in helping people help themselves. Beyond that—"

"Beyond that, you don't find me interesting in the slightest bit." He sounded wounded, and maybe he was. Thoughts of employment offers aside, he wanted to know why this one beguiling woman wasn't interested in the guy the *News and Observer* had hailed as "The Most Interesting Man in the State." Was she playing hard to get, or did he finally encounter an eligible young woman who didn't want him?

She crossed her legs toward the door and faced forward. "I don't know what to make of you. This guy here behind the steering wheel seems profoundly different than the one the press likes to follow around. Which one's the imposter?"

Huh?

"Well, they're both me, more or less. Maybe we should hang out and you can figure it out for yourself."

"I imagine you have plenty of people falling all over themselves to hang with you."

"And?" He slowed the car and made a right turn down a dirt road.

"Where are you going?"

"Oh, just checking out the struts."

She gave him that same blank expression. He figured she wouldn't know what a strut was, so it was a good enough lie for what he had in mind. Interview over. Damned woman. Yeah, he was pissed now. It actually bugged him the curvaceous runt hadn't thrown herself at his feet. Maybe he'd taken for granted that when he'd find a woman he was interested in enough to pursue, she'd actually be into him.

When they reached a dilapidated farmhouse and outbuildings, he said a little prayer to the god of debauchery and unfastened his seatbelt. "I'm just going to look at the radiator. Make sure it's not getting too hot." He pulled the handle and listened to the pop.

She shrugged. "Suit yourself."

"Thank you."

Once in front of the car, he hid in front of the open hood and brought up the messaging menu on his phone. "Okay, Tina. Here's the first one. Her business card reads Mandy McCarthy. Legal name is Miranda. Check under both names, will you? Last address was probably in Raleigh."

Twenty seconds later, Tina buzzed back. "Do these people know you're checking them out?"

"Nope."

"Are you trying to get me in trouble?"

"Look, I'll take care of the consent stuff, all right? I promise. I'm not going to get you into any shit."

"How deep do you want me to check?"

He rubbed the stubble on his chin as he thought about it. Normally, he only checked basic things like recent arrests, credit reports, and employment history. It didn't seem like enough. He sent: "Just do all the basic stuff. I'll find out the rest." The rest had nothing to do with her qualifications and more about his ego.

"And the others?"

"There's a tow operator named Frank Escondito. Originally from Long Beach. Definitely discontented and experienced in the way we need. Also, a Michael Leonard."

A long pause. "THE Michael Leonard? The motocross guy? That's the eye candy?! YUM."

He felt his face scrunch up with his confusion. *Who?* "I have no idea. Save that one for last. He's pretty charming and would be good in Chas's position, but he might be handful."

A handful in a different way he expected Mandy to be—the kind of handful that would *keep* him from Mandy. Those two seemed way too chummy for his liking. He made it a policy to not hire siblings, but rules were made to be broken, assuming the rewards offset the potential hassle.

"Got it. See you at two."

He forced a smile onto his face before slamming down the hood. Mandy was rooting around in her purse for something and the loud crash hadn't prompted her to look up. The woman obviously had nerves of steel.

Well, let's make her a little nervous.

He walked over to her door and pulled the handle.

"Hey, Mandy, can you step out of the car for a moment? I want to ask you something."

She stopped rooting and raised one eyebrow. "About the car?"

"No, sweetheart, the car is fine. I want to talk to you about your job."

"And we can't do that from inside the car?"

He shook his head. "Hey, I've got a brain. I need some space in case you decide you hate me and want to punch me in the nose."

"Oh, Jesus." She rolled her eyes, but unfastened her seatbelt.

After she'd gotten out and closed the door, he took a step closer.

She eyed him warily.

He took another step, close enough that he caught the scent of vanilla from her hair and the slight hint of musk that seemed ever-present on women during those hot Southern summers. One more step and they were toe to toe.

She leaned back against the car door and crossed her arms after lowering her sunglasses onto her nose. "Do you always have business conversations standing this close to people?"

"No."

"So how do I rate so high to get special treatment?"

Honesty, flattery, or straight-up lie? Which would work on a satin-haired enigma? He decided to start with flattery.

"I meant what I said earlier, Mandy. You're stunning."

A little flush met her cheeks and made her olive skin seem like lamps had been turned on underneath. "Thank you. But what does that have to do with my job?"

"We're talking about two different things here."

"Obviously the first is my job. What's the second?"

Slowly, he brought up his hands and brushed her hair from her collarbone, barely grazing her skin with the tips of his thumbs. When she didn't flinch or pull away, he put his lips where his fingers had been, grazing them along the satiny skin.

Impelled by her intoxicating aroma, he moved his mouth over the pulse point of her neck and licked as he put his hands at her waist.

"If you're trying to get a discount . . . " She sucked in some air. "You'll have to take that up with Archie. And I don't think this method works on him. He's not really into carnal favors."

He pulled her against him, mashing his swelling arousal against her belly and stilling her lips by pressing his against them. When her lips parted readily, he traced his tongue around them, not giving a single damn about her lipstick. Then he held her back and looked at her slack expression.

What a damned confusing woman.
"I take it you don't find me repulsive," he quipped.
"I never said I did. You didn't ask the right questions."
He nipped at her earlobe with his teeth, being very careful to avoid the pearl stud. Her whispered moan sent a surge of blood into his crotch. "Oh. What should I ask?" He kissed back down her jaw and returned to her mouth, which he hovered over awaiting her reply.
"Ask me if I'm attracted to you."
He felt the tips of her fingers digging into the fleshy part of his ass through his clothes. "Are you attracted to me, sweetheart?"
"Yes. Now ask me if I want to be involved." She traced her hands up his spine beneath his shirt, the softness of her palms making his gut clench.
He thought he knew the answer, but asked anyway. "Do you want to be involved?"
"Absolutely not."
He thought wrong. "Why the Hell *not?*"

*

Obviously not the answer he was expecting. Mandy straightened her clothes and used the side mirror to wipe her smeared lipstick off her chin. "We should be getting back to the lot."
"Yeah, we should. I've got paperwork to do and have a two-and-a-half hour drive to make a meeting, but I want you to answer my question. I can afford the time it'll take for you to give me the answer."
She pulled her door open and fell gracefully into the passenger seat, crossing her legs toward the left and cocking her head to the side.
He had his brow furrowed, and his face had gone all red.
Poor baby.

"Relationships always end abruptly for me, so I avoid them and anything resembling them."

"Are you kidding me?" He closed her door and jogged around the front of the sedan to the driver's side. When he'd buckled himself in and started the ignition, he picked up his wearying investigation again. "What does that mean, exactly? You don't even have sex?"

She gritted her teeth and talked through her clamped jaws. "That's a really personal question, Mr. Owen. Let's stick to business."

"*Aaron*. I think after I just nearly maimed you with my erection, you have standing permission to call me Aaron."

She looked at him and found his forehead still deeply set with worry lines. "*Aaron*."

After carefully backing down the long dirt path and putting the car on Highway 17, he said, "Look, I don't make a habit of mixing business and pleasure. You should be flattered."

She snorted and laughed so hard the button at the back of her tight skirt freed itself. "I'm sorry, did you just say I should be flattered? Bit cocky, aren't you?"

"No, this doesn't have anything to do with me being cocky. This has to do with how careful I am. When's the last time you saw me with a woman other than my mother or sister?"

"Like I told you before, I don't keep up. For all I know, you could seduce a woman at every used car lot in the state."

He cringed, and when a car passed in front of him too close to the front bumper he leaned on the horn. "You keep saying that, but I *don't*. Right now I'm only concerned with seducing one particular woman, but she's turning more and more into an ice cube with each passing minute."

She sighed and directed her gaze to the side window. *What a mess. This shit doesn't happen in real life.*

One of the other major faults she hadn't wanted to reveal to Aaron was that she got attached too easily. She couldn't just have sex with a guy and let him go on his way without some heartbreak. Heartbreak seemed inevitable from a guy like him. He was well off, had a stable nuclear family, and knew what he wanted to be when he grew up. Then there was the bit about how he could probably be cast as Prince Charming's stunt double in a live action filming of *Cinderella*. She'd seen pictures of his father, obviously, but Governor Owen wasn't that much of a looker. Aaron must have got it from his mother.

Have I ever seen her? She chewed the inside of her cheek as she thought. Time for a change of subject.

"You said you wanted to talk to me about my job. What of it?"

He was quiet as he navigated road curves and concentrated on passing a farm vehicle on the two-lane road. Finally, he explained. "Every now and then when I'm out doing business for the charity, I encounter people I think might be a good fit for my staff. It's how I've found some of my best folks. My most senior project manager, Tina, came out of a social services agency. I went in to do a presentation and came out with her business card and résumé. She's been with me since the start."

"And where do I fit in?"

"I thought earlier since you've been around cars a lot, you'd be good at what Tina does: she interviews families, consults with our tech guys to choose appropriate vehicles for them, and delivers them to the families we approve for the program."

"But now you realize my ineptitude, is that what you're saying?"

"No, not at all. I think now you'd be better suited for something else."

"Well, what?"

"Something that would force you to work very closely with me. The job I told you before I needed someone for. Someone to coordinate my staff, especially now that we're about to spread further into Virginia and South Carolina."

"What makes you think I'd be good at that?"

"I don't know, but I'm hoping. The job doesn't even have a formal description yet. It's just something I know I need."

"Interesting." She wasn't just blowing smoke. She was intrigued. The job would be a far cry from managing clothing stores, but the skill sets probably had some overlap. It was worth thinking about, at least. "Could I live anywhere?"

"Yeah, you could telecommute. We all meet once per month in Durham, though, so you'd have to keep that open. I'd prefer if you lived near the office."

"Why?"

"Because I live near the office."

Back to that again. She rolled her eyes.

"If you want, I can have Tina give you a call and let her tell you some more about what needs to be done?" His words were a statement, but the way his voice went up at the end made it sound more like a question.

"Okay, yeah. I may decide I'm not suitable for it, but I'd love to talk to her." Understatement, and she knew it. She would give her eyeteeth to move out of Archie's house.

"Awesome. I'll just need a bit of info before I go. We do a bit of screening before we get too serious about candidates and that way no one ends up disappointed." He gave her a cautious sideways look, probably expecting her to balk. She wouldn't. She'd been there. When she was managing Ermine's, she did her fair share of background checks on people. One could never be too careful.

"Fine."

He exhaled loud and long. "Do me a favor and don't say anything to Archie? I could use a guy like Frank in this part of the state and—"

"What?"

"Well, and Mike, too. He knows cars."

"You probably shouldn't worry too much about Mike. He's got another job lined up."

He furrowed his forehead again as he waited at the stoplight at the ramp onto Highway 32. "Good to know."

As soon as they pulled back into the lot, Archie emerged through the screen door and stood on the concrete block steps scowling.

She groaned. "Damn it, he threw the sale to Mike. He's probably pissed Mike didn't follow up."

Aaron reached across the console and squeezed her knee. Oddly, she wasn't inclined to swat it away.

"Don't worry about it. He's got nothing to bitch about. I'm buying the car."

"Thank fuck."

Mike came running, hobbling really, from the back lot and joined them at the hood after they disembarked.

"So, what do you think?"

"I'll take it," Aaron said.

"Good! Mandy, you want me to show you how to do the paperwork?"

Aaron gave Mike a manly thump on the back. "Hey, Mike, why don't you let Archie help with it? Can I talk to you for a second?"

All the air she'd been holding in her lungs blew out in one forceful exhalation. She whimpered at the prospect of yet another demoralizing exchange with the Archduke, but understood what Aaron was doing.

Suck it up, girlie. She smoothed the wrinkles from her skirt and walked to the trailer with a borrowed confidence energizing her steps.

"Guess what, Archie!" she said cheerfully when she was within range. "We've got a sale."

"Good for you," he said, pulling open the storm door and stepping through it. That was it.

She grunted her annoyance, but followed him into the

trailer. Who cared if Archie was cheerful? If Aaron's proposition shook out the way she hoped, and she'd just decided upon that spurning she'd pursue that chance to escape, her days at AA1A were numbered.

CHAPTER 5

Mandy thought that second blue drink had probably been a bad idea, but she'd had a moment of weakness. Her friend Chelsea's recounting of all the gossip she'd missed in the past couple of years had somehow affected her judgment. It was as if listening to all the inane chatter had transmogrified her brain into a gelatinous state. All she could do was sip and nod. Chelsea was still running her mouth, and Mandy tried to focus, but her eyes crossed from the potent combination of *Curaçao* and rum. Eventually, she just tuned her out.

"So, that about catches you up on all the Edenton drama." Chelsea twirled the end of her blonde braid around her finger and popped her nicotine gum. Mandy had tried explaining she wasn't supposed to chew it, much less try to blow bubbles with it, but Chelsea's only reaction had been a blank stare. At least she was trying to quit. Again.

"What's going on with you, lady?" Chelsea wrapped one arm around Mandy's waist and gave her a squeeze from her bar stool. "I'm so glad you're home."

Mandy scoffed into her blue drink. "I love catching up, Chels, and I missed you, too, but I plan on being on the first thing smoking out of here."

Her conversation with Tina had been energizing and left her feeling hopeful for a change. Then again, she'd been in an excellent mood since Aaron Owen had damn near impaled her out at the old farm. The last time she had felt so flattered was in fourth grade when Mrs. Edmund plucked her out of all the swaying daisies in the corps de ballet and promoted her above all the other girls to the role of bumblebee. She loved being the bumblebee. It was a role she thought was made for her. Her grandmother would agree.

Chelsea leaned her head onto Mandy's shoulder, her inebriated body swaying precariously on her perch. "Aww, I lub you." Chelsea sniffed. "I hate you for getting fired from Ermine's. Where am I going to get my discounted Sweet Louisa shit?"

"You'll have to order it online like the rest of the proletariat, babe." Mandy pulled her little leather Sweet Louisa clutch a bit further away from Chelsea's sticky reaching hand. If necessary, she would maim to protect that bag. It was from the fall sneak peek and the last thing she'd bought before getting the boot.

"Is that pretty Mandy out without her chaperone?"

She looked up into the bar mirror to find Dillon Slade idling near the tavern's front door, wearing a smile so big it could rival the moon for a moth's attention.

"Ew." She turned her shoulder too quickly without regard to Chelsea, causing the poor pickled lush to slip off her stool.

"Damn it," Chelsea mumbled listlessly and popped her gum again.

Mandy extended a hand to help her up.

Chelsea swatted it away. "Lemme sit here for juuuuuust a second." Her eyelids were heavy as she swayed and studied the laces of her pink Top-siders.

By the time Mandy straightened up, Dillon had spanned the distance between them and had his arms opened.

"Come on, Mirandy, you fox. Give us a hug."

She raised a brow. "Have you finally fallen off your rocker, Dillon? When did you start referring to yourself as plural?"

He enveloped her in a bear hug so forceful her feet cleared the floor by a foot. While he rocked her side by side, he said, "Aw, you're so funny. I forgot how funny you were."

She rolled her eyes. That was odd. He hadn't thought she was all that funny when he dumped her at eighteen right before she was due to leave for college. In fact, when he'd called her to end things his excuse had been that he didn't think there were enough sparks between the two of them. She had wondered what he could possibly know about sparks at eighteen, but in the end just shrugged it off. It probably wouldn't have lasted with her being in Chapel Hill and him down in Wilmington, anyway.

When he put her down, he held her in front of him as if she was a pay phone and he was trying to figure out where the quarter went.

She raised her other brow and stifled a scoff. "Like what you see?" she asked, assessing his polo shirt and khaki shorts, then scanning up to his spare chin, thin lips, and eyes that were too small for his round head.

Maybe "us" is appropriate since he's twice the man he used to be.

Once upon a time, he'd been attractive, but like so many other boys from her class, Dillon hadn't aged well. She'd dodged a bullet with that one. Compared to Aaron Owen, Dillon looked a lot like the catch that got thrown back. She felt her cheeks burn even thinking about Aaron and how he'd raised her body temperature to boiling in a matter of seconds.

Goddamn, that man's tongue. She pulled her collar away from her neck with the mere thought of his forthright advances. Guy didn't play around.

"Heck yeah!" Dillon chafed her arms with his hands and did a none-too-discreet scan of the tavern. "So, uh, where's Mike tonight?"

"He's at home icing and heating his knee, probably."

Dillon's smile widened a tick before he wrapped an arm around her shoulders. "Oh yeah? Sucks he got himself busted up so bad. Terrible pity. You, uh, want to have a drink?"

For once, she was thankful for Chelsea's sloppy drunkenness. She wasn't in the mood for Dillon's poorly targeted kisses, or for hearing the way he grunted when he was trying to get his face in just the right position. She shuddered at the thought. Any excuse to beg off would have been a good one. She offered him a consoling pat on the shoulder.

"Sorry, I won't be able to drive home if I have anything else."

His mouth twitched. He'd never been good at thinking on his feet. "Oh, that's okay. I'll drive you home."

"Uh . . . "

In high school, Dillon's vehicle had been a twenty-year-old pick-up truck. They'd spent numerous evenings under the stars in the open back "cuddling." She cringed to think back on all that awkward petting she thought was so hot at the time. Maybe *she* was just hot and didn't know the difference. Dillon would have just been a means to an end, but fortunately for her quarter-life self-esteem, things never progressed that far.

Yuck.

The pocket of her light jacket buzzed, and she held up one hand to the aged quarterback. "Just one moment." She plugged one finger into her ear and held the phone up to the other while making a beeline for the ladies' room.

"Whoever you are, I love you."

"I love you, too, Miranda," said a chuckling man with a deep baritone voice.

She stood in the corner by the settee patrons used to freshen their lipstick and fix their bra stuffing and squinted down at the phone display. It was an unknown number.

"Who's this?"

"It's Aaron. Aaron Owen. Your number was on your business card. I hope it's not too late to call. Am I interrupting anything?"

She sucked in a bit of air. The things that man's voice did to her should have been declared illegal on all continents. It reminded her of the hum of an engine: low with just a bit of purr at all the right times. It made her want to pin him down and squeeze his head between her thighs while he . . .

53

She yanked a length of paper towel from the dispenser, blasted cold water on it, and dabbed her brow.

Lord have mercy.

"Are you there?"

She tossed the paper and paced in front of the settee once more. "Yes, sorry. I'm here. No, you're not interrupting. I'm just with a friend."

"I won't hold you up, then. I just wanted to see if you got in touch with Tina. She's a bit of a moving target and I wanted to know if you had any questions or comments before tomorrow."

"Oh!" She straightened her blouse as if he could see it, then thunked herself on the forehead with the heel of her palm when she realized what she was doing. "Yes, we spoke earlier."

"Good. I'll let you sleep on it all. I guess I'll see you at the lot tomorrow?"

"Yes."

"'Night, then."

"Right. Goodnight."

She stuffed her phone back into her pocket and paced some more. Then she giggled. "Shit, I am screwed. He's gonna use me up for sure."

When she pulled the bathroom door open, still mumbling to herself, she found Dillon stood on the threshold. He took a step back to let her out.

"Dillon, you really didn't have to wait for me here."

Weirdo. Ew. Was that really the best I could do in twelfth grade?

"Oh, I know. I just didn't want you to miss seeing me. Here I am!"

She chuckled and it came out sounding forced, even to her ears. "Yeah. There you are, guy."

Chelsea had managed to get upright once more and held her arm out, snapping her fingers to get the bartender's attention. Mandy decided the fates were on her side for once. Who was she to piss off the fates? Best she listen.

"Shit, Dill. You know what? I need to get Chelsea home before she drinks herself sick. She didn't drive."

"Hell, she doesn't live that far. She could probably walk."

She shook her head and put her hands on her hips. "I wouldn't send her out in the condition she's in. She'd probably trip over a crack in one of those old sidewalks and smash that cute little elfin nose of hers all to smithereens. Hey—"

She patted his chest right in the middle and gave him a bland smile.

"Nice seeing you."

"I'll call you?"

She nodded. "Sure. You do that." She gave a little finger wave before turning on the heel of her ballet flat and walking with purpose to the bar.

Chelsea was still snapping her fingers at the bartender when Mandy got there. Mandy grabbed her by the arm.

"Hey, Chels? There's a smokin' hot guy on a motorcycle outside asking about you."

Chelsea's unfocused brown eyes went wide. "Really? Asking for *me?*" She slid off the barstool and let Mandy lead her out.

"Mm hmm. *You*, babe."

CHAPTER 6

Aaron pushed his peas around on his plate and tried to tune out the chattering around him. He hated those scheduled family dinners at the governor's mansion. At age thirty, they felt far too much like edicts than actual invitations, but somewhere deep down inside he knew if it weren't for those dinners, he'd never see his family at all. Also deep down, he was uncertain if he cared.

When a hard dinner roll bounced off his shoulder and onto the tabletop in front of him, he looked up from his unimpressive meal to find Elly making a *'Well'* face at him. Good enough excuse to put his fork down. He'd only been pretending to eat, anyhow.

"I'm sorry, did you ask me something, El?"

Elly rolled her eyes in the patented Elizabeth Owen double-swirl. "Yes, I asked if you had an opinion about that magazine article."

"Magazine? What magazine? I don't even read magazines. Who reads magazines?"

"See Rick!" Her voice was jubilant as she turned to their father's closest aide and campaign manager and stabbed her index finger in his general direction. "He doesn't even know what I'm talking about."

"I rarely know what you're talking about so that's a poor debate point. What's going on now?"

She rolled her brown eyes yet again and flipped her long, straight hair from one naked shoulder over to the other.

The gesture made thoughts of Mandy, whom he'd been trying his damnedest to forget about all evening, crowd out every other. When Mandy flipped her hair, she had a sort of casual elegance that indicated she didn't really care if she was being watched; the flip was a factor of utility. Elly's flips were all about the attention. Then again, most everything about Elly was about attention.

She was chaos bound together by skin and bone, and the thorn in their father's side. It was because of her love affair with the press that Aaron couldn't date without scrutiny. She liked her men to come with their own measure of notoriety: movie stars, rock musicians, athletes, wealthy heirs, and so on. The more issues they had, the better she liked them. She seemed to thrive on controversy and getting her to keep her mouth shut whenever a reporter shoved a microphone into her face was an impossible task. With all the interest in the pretty blonde whose father might be president in a few years, Aaron was collateral damage.

"The article in *OK!* about my last overseas trip. Rick says it's scandalizing and embarrassing. Isn't that what you said, Rick?" Elly broke off a piece of her roll and threw it at him.

"It is!" Rick barked, color flooding his cheeks as he swatted the bread away.

Aaron blew out a breath and pushed his hair behind his ears.

Rick and Elly had the same damn argument every dinner he was in attendance for, which was part of the reason he avoided them. When would the man learn to give it up? Rick would have made more headway thrashing his face against a concrete wall.

"What were you doing in the pictures?" Aaron asked, voice weary.

Elly shrugged and flaked her salmon with her fork.

His mouth watered. Compared to the veg-something on his plate he hadn't been able to identify, the fish looked like the gateway to Shangri-La. It was as if he'd offended the chef, somehow, although for the life of him he couldn't imagine when it'd been. Never once had he had a palatable entrée at the executive mansion although everyone else seemed to be doing just fine. The way Aaron figured it, food should be edible, whether it had once breathed or not.

"Kissing some ambassador's son," Elly continued. "I don't even know his name." Her lips twitched at the corners.

Mom, at the other end of the table, sighed loudly. When Aaron looked down the table, he saw she'd buried her face in her hands.

Rick pounded the tabletop. "Carter Patel, for Chrissake!" He leaned sideways to spot Aaron around the large floral centerpiece. "Help me out here, Aaron. You've got to do something—find her some couth; I don't care if you have to buy it. At the rate she's going, your father won't be nominated by his own party for re-election! Who would want to nominate someone who can't keep a leash on his own kid?"

Aaron gritted his teeth and turned knots in the cloth napkin he held beneath the table. *Leash, huh?* He counted to five in his head before speaking.

"Rick, she's twenty-three. Hardly a child. She has a college degree, even. If she wants to tart around, it's really not my problem. Nor is it yours."

Elly balked. "I'm not a tart!"

"Kiddo, I know you're not. That's the perception, and perception is everything in politics. Not reality. I know you're an incorrigible flirt, but I imagine most people don't see your serial dating in the same light as folks who know you."

"Listen to your brother, Elly, if not Rick." That was from Mom, who was already halfway into her third glass of muscadine wine. She'd grumbled when she had the kitchen staff open the cloyingly sweet stuff, but some Piedmont-area chamber of commerce had forwarded it to her and they had a tendency to follow up on that kind of thing. She needed an opinion other than, "It made me drunk. I liked it." So, she was trying to formulate an opinion, one bottle at a time.

Elly used her lips in the best impersonation of a motorboat Aaron had heard since elementary school. "As if! I'm not going to cloister myself just because Dad is holding office. No one asked me what I thought before he decided to drop his name into the hat. I'm not going to hide out and play pretend. My sorority sisters think this is a goddamned riot."

Dad set down his fork and knife and knit his brows. "Language, Elly!"

Aaron's thoughts darted to Mandy, the woman whose swearing was so fluent she could make a bawdy sea shanty sound like a lullaby. He wanted to smack himself for that lame-ass attempt at a conversation he'd initiated earlier over the phone. All his charm seemed to evaporate when she was the object of his attention. She must have thought he was some kind of boorish dolt, coming onto her the way he had.

Elly swirled her eyes around in their sockets once more and swatted a hand toward the end of the table. "Oh, come off it, Dad. I was an adult when you ran for this ticket and I was scared enough of you then that I stayed out of public view until you were safely inaugurated. Well, I'm twenty-three, Guv'nor. I'm a college graduate. I can do what I want." She did a little dance in her seat that actually made Aaron laugh.

She's fearless. I'll give her that.

When Mom shot a glare in his direction, he cleared his throat and focused on his . . . well, he didn't know what it was on his plate, but he looked at it.

Rick scoffed. "An unemployed college graduate. Who do you think finances all those trips and escapades you like to go on with your sorority sisters, huh?"

"That's a good point, Rick." Dad returned his attention to his dinner and speared a floret of broccoli with his fork.

Aaron growled, both from hunger and annoyance. *Why the Hell don't I have broccoli?*

He was nearly salivating over his father's manipulation of the vegetables on his plate when his mother's fingertips drumming against the tabletop pulled his focus away.

She cocked her head to the side and gave him a blank expression he pretended not to see.

"I'm cutting you off until you shape up, Elly. No more allowance," Dad said.

Aaron scoffed. Between Elly's trust fund and what she had in savings, she'd hardly go hungry. She wouldn't even have to nick her manicure clipping coupons. It was the same reason he managed to get by while his CTW salary was just a hair over minimum wage.

"Furthermore, consider your car repossessed until further notice."

That got her attention, and Aaron's, too. She peeled her upper lip back into a sneer and threw her linen napkin in Dad's direction.

"What the Hell do you expect me to do? Take the bus around Raleigh? Yeah. Right. I'll just buy a new one."

Dad kept eating, obviously unmoved. "Maybe you should take the bus. You'd learn something about the people I serve."

"Right, the people *you* serve, Daddy. I'm one of them—a goddamned constituent, and as of right now, you wouldn't get my vote. I'm not trying to ride your coattails. I don't give a hot damn about politics. In fact, I don't even care that much about North Carolina." She tossed her napkin onto the table and studied her nails. "I'm moving back to Europe."

"Great, you do that. When's the last time you saw your license and passport?"

Elly's jaw dropped. "Excuse me?"

"It means," Rick volunteered, "I confiscated your travel documents last week."

Her face flushed like the ripe muscadines used in Mom's wine. She clamped her jaw, stuck out her lips, and gripped the edge of the table. When she stood and yanked at the tablecloth, nearly half of the dishes on her side crashed to the floor. "You were going through my things? My *purse*? My apartment?"

Aaron whistled low and placed his utensils on the table before standing. He figured he should get home to ensure his own private documents hadn't been riffled through.

"Where are you going, Aaron?" Dad didn't even look up from his pilaf.

Why didn't I get pilaf?

"I'm going home. Don't drag me into this shit. I behave for the cameras, and you have no idea what I give up to do so."

Things like Mandy.

"Don't sling Elly's problems onto me, too. I've got enough frustrations of my own."

Dad remained nonplussed. "If I'm not mistaken, isn't Cars to Work funded at least in part by a state grant?"

Mom buried her face into her hands again and groaned. "Oh, don't go there, Charles."

Aaron cracked his knuckles and let his fists fall to his sides. "I applied for that grant the same way everyone else had to. I filled out all the goddamned forms, submitted all the verifying documents, waited months for an answer just like everyone else. I didn't get any special treatment. You had nothing to do with it."

Dad reached for his highball glass. "That may be so. Still, it'd be a shame if you suddenly became ineligible next year, especially when you're in the midst of expanding."

Aaron laughed and shook his head, disbelieving. "You see this, Mom? This is exactly why I don't dick around in politics, and the next time some reporter asks me about my ambitions, I'm going to tell them exactly that. Doesn't matter which side you're on. After a while, you'll do whatever you need, con whomever you need to get your way—even in your private life. I don't want to be that kind of person. So, do what you have to do, Dad. And also? Fuck you very much."

He had made it all the way out to his SUV and had his key in the ignition when he looked up into the rearview mirror to find

Mom dragging Elly out by the arm. He locked the doors and started the engine. Mom ran up to his door and knocked on the glass. He motored down the window.

"What?"

"First of all, shame on you for talking to your father like that. Second, please take Elly with you."

"You're right, I'm sorry for the language. But, no."

He mashed the button to put the glass back up.

"Aaron! *Please*. Just for a few days while I deal with this mess."

He took his finger off the button. "Mom, I really can't. Even if I wanted to, which I don't, I can't. I have to be back out in Chowan early tomorrow morning. I have work to do. Meetings to attend. I don't have time to babysit. Besides, last I checked, Elly was a grown-ass woman."

"Aaron, I need you to be the big brother again. Take her! Keep her in the car if you have to."

Elly's jaw dropped. "I'm not a puppy!"

Mom gave Elly a silencing pinch of the forearm. "For God's sake, Aaron. Have some mercy."

He dug his pen out of his back pocket and spun it between his fingers. "Why? Why is this so important all of a sudden?"

She closed her eyes and held in a breath for a long while. When she opened her eyes again, he realized they were bloodshot. What'd been going on in the Owen household?

"I know this is hard for both of you, being under the microscope like this. You didn't ask for it."

"Quit beating around the bush, Mom. What kind of trouble is Elly in this time? Did she smuggle antiquities out of a foreign country again?"

"That was an accident!" Elly squeaked.

"Nothing like that. Please, just keep her under the radar for a couple of days. Maybe head back to the beach house?"

"No way. There are cameras there now, did you know that?

Hope Dad enjoyed me sitting on my ass watching G4 all last week. I bet it was a good show."

"Damn it, I didn't know that." She slumped. "Look, it doesn't matter where, just *take* her until your aunt can collect her in Southport."

"*Collect* her? What the Hell is going on here?"

Mom put up a shaking hand. "Please stop asking questions."

He studied her face—its worried lines and the tiredness in her eyes—and blew out a breath. Whatever it was she was contending with, she didn't deserve it. Her life had been turned upside down by the governor's ambitions, too. She was a quiet woman who'd grown up the daughter of a Methodist minister father and a fabric shop owner mother. He knew this wasn't the life she would have chosen for herself.

"Yeah." He toggled the locks.

Mom yanked the back door open, tossed her sullen offspring into the backseat, and flicked a credit card at him.

He flicked it back. "I don't need that."

She tossed it back through the window and took two steps back. "Take it. I know what you pay yourself." She walked around to the other side of the car and opened that door to toss the plain black backpack she'd been wearing into the footwell behind the passenger seat. After slamming the door, she set off for the back door of the mansion without looking back.

He watched Elly yank on the door handle on one side then the other to no avail.

"Goddamn it, she put the child safety locks on."

CHAPTER 7

"Aaron, you can't just leave the poor girl in the car like that. It's hot as shhh-*sugar* outside." Mandy cut her eyes toward Mike, but he was too busy entertaining the jailed Elly through the back window of the SUV to pay attention to her. She lowered her voice to a whisper. "And thanks for not ratting me out to Mike."

Aaron looked affronted. "Hey, I'm no snitch!" He spread on that smile that made Mandy fear for the structural integrity of her panty elastic.

She swallowed down the boulder-sized lump forming in her throat, only to feel her stomach revolt at the sudden addition of a heaping handful of fresh nerves. The man cleaned up good, and it affected her. It affected her a *lot*. Maybe it was her clothing store background, but a man who knew how to buy slacks that actually fit really turned her on. The fact he actually had an ass didn't hurt, either. It was far more evident in his belted black slacks than it'd been in the baggy shorts he'd worn the day before, although she did recall there being a bit of flesh there when she'd squeezed. She ran her tongue over her lips involuntarily before catching herself.

He mirrored the act and pushed his sunglasses to the top of his head to fix his hazel gaze on her.

She suddenly felt a bit faint, and walked away fanning her face with her hands. Retreating was cowardly, but she didn't care. Her pride was at stake and she was being sucked into a goddamned black hole of charisma. She made a beeline for a station wagon three rows over and squatted down next to the back tire on the far side, putting her head between her knees before commencing with a deep breathing exercise.

He's not for you. Don't touch him. He's not for you. Don't touch him.

She kept repeating the mantra in her mind, over and over again until she was reasonably certain she could deflect his charms. When she stood, he was still leaning against the front of his SUV, looking in her direction with an eyebrow cocked.

Well, get on with it.

She waved him over. It was as good a time as any.

"This car came in from an auction yesterday," she said, trying for a confident tone, but sounding like a clarinet with a bad vibrato.

He grunted and bent down to stare into the window. "What can you tell me about it?"

She cleared her throat and felt her blood pressure ebb. As long as they kept the conversation on business, she could deal. "Not a damn thing other than the fact it's a Volvo."

"Hey, that's a lot."

"Liar." She folded her arms over her breasts as he stood and smiled at her.

Don't touch him. He's not for you!

"I told you I'm hopeless with cars." She backed up a few paces toward the trunk to get out of his field of gravity. "I can't tell one model year apart from another if they're within five years."

"It's okay. You're cute when you're hopeless."

Her cheeks burned. He just had to go there. "Only when I'm hopeless, huh?"

He lifted his broad shoulders in a dramatic shrug and made his grin even broader. "Drive it?"

"Absolutely," she said, glad for the distraction.

He caught the key she tossed at him and shifted the front seat back to accommodate his long legs. "Same place as yesterday?" His eyes cast downward to the low V-neck of her dress.

She worked her lips from one side of her face to the other and stole a glance over to the trailer. Archie was at his window again. She gave him a little wave. Archie shook his head and walked away.

"Why, think you need to test the struts?"

"Yeah, your struts."

"You don't hash words, do you?"

He shrugged. "We know where this is going."

"We're going to drive down Highway 17 so you can put some stress on the engine of this grocery-getter."

"That's all, huh?"

She closed his door and harrumphed before walking around the hood of the car.

So many mixed signals. Does he want to employ me or lay me? He can't have both, can he?

She pondered that while pulling open the front passenger door. Was there a law against fraternization or did management types just strongly recommend against it? She'd never encountered the situation when she was at Ermine's. As far as she could tell, none of the staff had been that kind of friendly to each other. She certainly didn't get on like that with the store's co-general manager. He was a married man with two grown kids and a pack-a-day smoking habit that made his hands smell like an ashtray.

She took one more peek at the office window and found Archie's distended belly pressed against it. His arms were crossed over his chest and he was wearing a scowl that could cut glass. She opted out of stoking the angry bull's temper for once, and just got into the passenger seat of the car.

Aaron started pulling out before she even had her seatbelt fastened.

"Aaron, I think Archie may suspect something. Mike isn't his favorite son, but still he's usually pleasant to him. Last night at dinner he was downright surly to the guy. When Mike asked him to pass the creamed corn, Archie nearly flung it across the table."

"Think Mike said something to him?"

"Doubt it. Mike keeps a secret really well, so I don't think he would have told Archie you're trying to recruit his best guy. He did seem like his interest was piqued. Mike, I mean. We talked about it a bit before I went out."

The clench of his jaw tightened, but Mandy didn't know what part of what she'd said had prompted his annoyance. Not that she understood men all that well, anyway. Maybe she was reading things into the situation that weren't there.

"That's good to hear, I guess," he said as he focused his attention on the highway. "He said it'd take a lot to get him to back out on the job offer he's already accepted, but if I could sweeten the pot a bit he'd reconsider. Speaking of sweet pots, tell me about how you felt about what you discussed with Tina last night? Sorry for interrupting your evening, by the way."

She shifted in her seat and smoothed the hem of her dress over her knees. "Don't worry about that. I ended up taking my friend home early. She was trashed."

"Hmm." His jaw relaxed when he turned down onto that bumpy dirt road once more.

They were quiet until they the car was far enough down the path to be out of sight from the highway. He cracked the windows and turned off the ignition.

"Tell me what you thought?" He pulled his silver-plated pen out of his dress shirt's pocket and spun it between those long, sun-kissed fingers.

She fixated on that strong hand, imagining all the places she would have him put it.

He's not for you, don't touch him.

She cleared her throat and crossed her legs in the other direction. "I was intrigued. It sounds like an interesting opportunity."

He unbuckled his seatbelt and put his back against the door. "That's the lame-ass politically correct brush-off line. Tell me what you really thought, Miranda."

God, did she love the sound of her name from his lips. If he were to whisper it in her ear, she'd likely combust. She pushed her bangs back from her eyes and risked a glance at him. He grinned, so she turned toward her window again.

"I don't have a problem with the job. It sounds great, actually. Perfect for me. I'd get to flex some of my managerial muscles and maybe develop some new ones. And it's not like I'm going to find another store to hire me." She added that last bit in a mumble.

"But?"

"But I have some concerns about whether or not I'd be able to get along with my boss."

"Concerns" was putting it mildly, considering the tawdry dreams she'd had the night before. They'd made her wake up with a soaked shirt and a sudden compulsion to drop to her knees and beg God not to smite her where she lay, because really? She thought they'd probably get along just fine . . . with her bent over his desk, or maybe in a locked supply closet, or . . .

He nodded and straightened up to push his door open without a word. When he appeared at the passenger door, she held her breath waiting for him to drop the first shoe.

"We get along perfectly well." He reached into the car, wrapped his fingers around her waist, and gave her a gentle but firm pull out of the seat to press her body against his.

She let out an embarrassing little squeak at his hardness pressed between them.

"Don't you agree?" He dragged his fingers down her hips to crumple the fabric of her dress up higher and higher. Once her thighs were exposed, he eased his knee between them, widening her stance, and stimulating her lace-covered crotch.

"I'm undecided. I think we have the wrong wires crossed here. I want the job, but we can't be having sex on the side. What would people think?"

He brought his mouth down to hers and teased his tongue in between her parted lips. Obviously she wasn't putting up a very effective blockade. Hell, she'd let the enemy in close without even so much a warning shot off his bow.

He threaded his fingers through her hair, holding her face firm against his, giving her no leeway, although she didn't really want any. What girl in her right mind would slip away from Aaron Owen? She'd thought she'd be the one to resist him because she had to, but fuck if it wasn't impossible.

His lips bore a hint of flavor from the black coffee he'd politely sipped at Archie's behest. Combined with the musky notes of his cologne and the slight undercurrent of motor oil he'd had the previous day, too, the effect was all masculine—Aaron's special brand of it.

When his fingers breached her panty elastic and rough palms abraded the delicate skin of her abdomen, she put her head back even more and breathed out a shaky breath.

"People aren't going to think anything, sweetheart." He slid his hands up her back and around her ribcage to the base of her breasts. "They're not going to know"

What?

It took every ounce of willpower she had, but that admonition was the spur she needed to swim out of her haze. She placed her hands against his chest and gave him an ineffectual little shove backward. He was just too damned big for her to get much leverage.

"I don't want to play secret lovers with you, Aaron. I'm one of those girls who gets easily attached, and this—" She indicated their disheveled states. "This is a recipe for disaster."

"You're thinking too hard, Miranda." He drew her close once more, this time slipping the neckline of her dress down with the edge of her bra to expose one nipple. His hot tongue danced over it as her worked his free hand up the back of her dress and into her panties.

She whimpered when his finger breeched her aroused sex. "Stop it! That's not fair."

"It's not meant to be. I want you, Miranda. I'll take what I can get."

"I think you could do a lot better than feeling me up in an overgrown field."

"You're right." He licked across the valley of her cleavage and paused at the lacy boundary covering her other breast. "You deserve better, but I don't know how to do this anymore. Especially not with all the constraints I've got against me."

"Do what? What is it you don't know how to do?" Her voice was breathy, because he had dropped to his knees there on the grass and lifted the bottom of her dress.

He gave perfect eye contact while hooking a finger into the wet crotch of her panties. "Date."

"Oh. I don't think this counts as a date." *Not unless I've been doing it wrong all these years.*

"No, it doesn't." He nudged backward her a few inches so her rear was against the passenger-side front door. When he wrapped his strong fingers around her ankle and pulled her foot free of her panties she had to grip the car behind her to keep her legs from going to jelly beneath her. Next, he put her leg over his shoulder and looked up at her with a dare in his eyes. "This madness you're currently experiencing is the result of you wearing that tight skirt yesterday and the way your thighs looked through the slit when you bent over."

He flicked a finger over her clit.

She whimpered.

"And that shirt you were wearing. Oh, sweetheart, that shirt. It's amazing what a little water can do for the imagination." He teased her with one slow, circular lick, touching nothing that mattered but causing her sex to clench with anticipation all the same.

"Jesus." She blew out a shuddering breath and strengthened her grip on the side mirror's stem. "And what do I get tomorrow for wearing this dress today?"

The more accurate question should have been "What am I going to do to you tomorrow for you wearing those slacks today." Crouched in front of her as he was, she could see his impressive thigh muscles flexing and clenching as he asserted his control over her body. And control it was. She wouldn't dare move.

"I don't know. Maybe you need a spanking. If it looks that good to me, it probably does to every other guy, too. That won't do." He flicked his tongue at her pert nub and smiled when she whimpered.

"Why not?"

"When you work for me, I'll have you kitted out in the finest sackcloth and burlap money can buy. That should keep the jackals from ogling you." He took it wholly into his mouth and sucked it as if it were a honeysuckle flower filled with sweet nectar.

She managed to ease her death grip on the car and raked her fingers through his thick hair, clamping her fists in it and holding on for dear life when he slipped two fingers into her. He didn't seem to mind the pulling, and she wondered if having his hair yanked was a common occurrence for him.

"I haven't agreed to work for you yet." The job hardly seemed relevant at the moment.

He obviously agreed, because he continued tormenting her clit with his tongue and didn't ease up until her legs began to wobble. She hissed his name and pulled his head back by the hair to force his face up to meet hers.

"Damn you."

"Damn me, huh?" He scissored his fingers inside, creating a delicious pressure that had her motor running once more. "Oh, it's only a matter of paperwork, sweetheart. Just tell me why you got fired from your last job."

"What?" She dropped her leg from his shoulder, swatted his hand—with some reluctance, there—and planted the sole of her

71

espadrille on his shoulder. He didn't move a hair from her prod. "That's really none of your business."

He raised one of those golden brown eyebrows and pushed his sunglasses back onto his nose. "Isn't it? I'm trying to offer you a job, here."

"Seems like you're trying to do a lot more than that." She found her panties in the grass and shook them out while Aaron got to his feet and wiped the grass off his knees.

"You're right. I'm not denying that."

"And you don't find this strange in the slightest bit?" she asked while pulling the passenger door open. She climbed into her seat without waiting for the answer.

He lowered his head into the open doorway. "I'm not contesting that, sweetheart. I agree it's an unusual circumstance. I want to hire you, and I want to make love to you. Why pick one over the other?"

Make love, he said. Make love! She harrumphed.

He was brazenly staring into her cleavage yet again, so she crossed her arms over her chest. "And how many other women have you hired that way? Hell of a signing bonus, right? Getting to screw the boss?"

That beaming smile. He was laughing at her.

She vowed to make him pay for it.

"None. I learned in kindergarten to keep my hands to myself. I learned sometime after that to keep everything about my business aboveboard. Transparent. Given the circumstances with my father being who he is, I tend to have extra incentive to keep my nose clean."

"But not your tongue."

"Funny. I like you, Miranda. I think I'll keep you."

She rolled her eyes and crossed her legs at the knees. Traitorous body! The idea of being kept by a man that sexy was a pretty damn heady thing, but experience had taught her that eventually, they all got bored. They all dumped her.

She clamped her thighs a bit tighter. "Are you buying this car or not?"

"Yes."

"Super."

When he was in the driver's seat again and had his seatbelt pulled across his lap, he turned the air conditioner up high and started to carefully turn a U in the field. Once well on the way to AA1A, he put his right hand on her thigh and gave it a squeeze. When she didn't object, he whispered, "I think you'll say yes."

She looked over to find his expression an absolute blank. "To what?"

"Anything I want, sweetheart."

CHAPTER 8

"I slipped the paperwork to Mike when Archie was running photocopies. He said he'd put it in your car." Aaron slammed the door of the wagon shut and used the clicker to lock it. He'd parked it next to the sedan he bought the day before. Archie, kind generous soul he was, offered to let Aaron store his purchased vehicles there for a fee of forty bucks per car per day until the Cars to Work team could collect and deliver them. There were two more cars he was interested in—a couple of small fuel-efficient hatchbacks great for young singles—that Archie couldn't find the titles for. He told him to come back. Aaron was glad to if it meant another chance to see Mandy, even if had to endure being the victim of a shakedown.

What a little firecracker she was. On one hand, she seemed to have a well-calibrated sense of self-worth. She knew she was better than what he was offering her: she deserved being wined and dined, not getting groped in the great outdoors. On the other hand, he'd managed to confuse the poor girl's sensors enough he might be able to make her do something she'd regret.

Every time he was near her, his thoughts went to a place far from gentlemanly. He wanted to consume her: for her to deliver herself to him mind, body, and soul, even if she had to remain his secret. How long was *that* going to work? If she'd been a guy, her answer would have been "five minutes." Just long enough to get off and put his shorts back on.

"I usually like an answer within twenty-four hours. Most folks give me a reply on the spot."

She pushed her bangs back with her sunglasses and turned her gray gaze to the office window Archie was standing behind. "Don't call me, I'll call you."

"Not necessary. I'll be here tomorrow with Tina and some of the other staff. They're going to deliver the cars before we head to a training event in Suffolk. We'll be there a couple of days, and it'd be a great way for you to meet everyone if you can make it. Get your feet wet, you know?"

She twirled a length of her hair around her index finger. "I'll think about it."

"Right. Go ahead and pack that bag." He winked and went to fetch Elly from the hospitality lounge where she'd retreated to watch soap operas at Archie's bequest. Once in the trailer, he handed his charge back her phone. She sat up fast and snatched it, immediately scrolling through the missed calls and messages.

"Ready to go?"

Elly grunted, nodded, and stood—all without looking up from her phone display. Her thumbs were working frantically over the keypad and she walked toward the door with an unusual sense of spatial awareness while texting away. "Did you read any of my messages?"

He held the storm door open for her and held his breath until she was safely down the stairs. "No. And by the way, Rick has access to your cell phone records. Whoever you're texting? Stop."

She froze there in front of a yellow VW bug with her jaw hanging open. "What?"

"Duh, Elly. If it's just one of your girlfriends, it's no big deal. Carry on." He lowered his voice and leaned in close. "But if I were you, I'd consider that phone a secret weapon that'll be deployed at any moment now. Do what I do. Get a phone that can't be tracked back to you if you need to make personal calls."

She stared down at the slick silver thing that was her life in plastic and electrons and pulled her upper lip back with a scoff. "I hate this family."

"That's nice, kiddo. Get in the damned truck."

"Where are we going now?"

He scanned the lot and found Mandy watching them from the far end where she was stood with Mike. He gave them a little salute, which Mike returned.

She pretended she didn't see him.

He ground his teeth.

"I'm taking you to Tina's for the night. She'll get you down to CTW in the morning, then you'll spend the next two days sitting in on a bunch of boring teambuilding exercises and administrative meetings. Might be good for you. Educational, even."

"Whoopie."

Whoopie, indeed. By the time he parked his SUV in front of the CTW office the next morning, Tina had texted or called no less than ten times encouraging him to "Speed it up!" for the sake of her fragile sanity. Apparently, Elly had spent the bulk of the night asking the poor woman hypothetical relationship questions and when Tina turned her back or blinked for longer than a microsecond, Elly was at the door trying to sneak out. Tina had resorted to corralling the petulant young woman into the master bedroom, which had no secondary exit, and sleeping on a pallet in the hallway.

"You don't pay me enough for this," Tina said to him the moment he unlatched the locks. He shrugged and watched her help Elly, dressed ever so appropriately for the trip in terrycloth booty shorts with *Hustla* printed in big white bubble letters on the ass, up into the middle seat. Tina took the spot to her right, and Eleanor sandwiched her in from the left. When he looked up into the rearview mirror, he found his little sister wearing a death glare.

He was unmoved.

Chas, Aaron's lifelong friend and one of his most savvy procurement guys, climbed up into the front passenger seat and slammed the door. "Holy Hell, man. Don't send me out to the mountains again without Eleanor. Those people think I'm a grade A sucka."

Aaron laughed. It wasn't the first time the folks out in the Appalachians had given him the runaround. "What happened this time?"

"I got all the way out to Murphy, right? There was supposed to be this big used car lot where I could get a bunch of cars for a steal. A few folks at a diner I stopped at for breakfast told me about it when I asked if they knew where I could find some good cars for cheap. Well, got out there and it turned out to be one stop above chop shop. A lot of those cars didn't even have VIN numbers on them, and trust me—I looked everywhere. I'm pretty sure they were trying to set me up."

"So you're telling me the trip was a complete bust?"

"Nope. I managed to pick up a little Nova off this old lady who had only driven it on Sundays for twenty years. It's stick shift, but folks out in the mountains like those. I left your paperwork in your inbox. Listen, you have any luck finding someone to take my place? I don't know how much longer my old man is going to forgive me for being out of the law office. You know I love being a part of the team and shit, but he's pretty vocal. I'm tired of the headaches."

Aaron groaned. *Fuck. Mike Leonard, throw me a bone, man.* "Chas, I'm working on it. It's not like I can replace you with a highly trained monkey. Besides, monkeys are expensive."

*

"Now that's more like it."

Mandy rolled her eyes at the sound of Aaron's voice and turned her attention back to his bustling staff. The female mechanic was making some notes on a clipboard about two older minivans. The guy Chas followed Tina out in Aaron's SUV as she left to deliver the station wagon. Elly was in the hospitality lounge being entertained by Mandy's mother, who sometimes hung out on the lot on the days she wasn't on the schedule at the hospital. She had nothing better to do.

"I assure you, my clothing choice today has absolutely nothing to do with you," she said in response to his quip. Her attire for the day consisted of wide-leg jeans and a plain black tank top. "I happen to be backed up on laundry."

In other words, Archie blocked the machine the night before and told her she'd have to pay three dollars per load.

"I'd hate to see what else you have in that laundry pile if Monday's and yesterday's attire are representative samplings."

"Definitely representative." She lifted her shoulders in a shrug. "I like clothes."

"Right." He pulled his pen out of the front pocket of his spring green button-up shirt and twirled it. "Well, what do you have on under them?"

She laughed and couldn't help it. His expression was so friendly, but his voice dripping with so much suggestion, the disparity was hard to ignore. And she'd tried ignoring him since the moment he'd driven onto the lot that morning, but that damned infuriating man kept chiseling little cracks into her exterior.

"Can't you guess? You've already seen an example of at least half my lingerie preferences."

"I'd rather see. I'm a visual learner."

She felt her blood start to surge and covered her chest with her arms. It definitely wasn't cold outside, but her nipples sure looked like it. "Nothing to be done about that."

"I don't know." He gave her shoulder a little nudge and pointed to the gray sedan he and Eleanor had deliberated over immediately after arrival. Structurally, it was okay. Interior was fair. There was a crack in the radiator Archie claimed he didn't know was there. Aaron thought he could talk him down on price a bit. Eleanor thought he'd lose whatever he'd save by haggling when fixing the radiator problem. "Go for a drive?"

She started to tingle down below even as the little voice in the back of her mind reminded *Don't touch him. He's not for you.*

"Aaron, I think that would complicate things a bit."

"How so? How are they going to get much more complicated than they already are? I mean, I've French kissed your Victoria's Secret."

As if she could forget.

She glanced at the office window, found no one in it for once, and grabbed him by the hand. "Come here." She pulled him around to the side of the trailer that faced a fallow cornfield, out of view of the folks on the main lot. Her intention had just been to hustle him from one place to the next for some added privacy, but when she got there, she didn't want to let go of his hand. It just felt right, her small one in his large rough one. With some difficulty she let it drop.

"I'm going to take the job. I'm pretty sure Archie has been angling to replace me regardless of the warning he gave. I heard him talking about it with my mother last night."

"That sounds sort of double-crossing, not that I can get upset about it since it benefits me."

She toyed with a button on his shirt and shrugged. "I don't think Mom knows the full extent of what's going on here. When Archie tells her little half-truths, she doesn't question him on them. She never questions him on anything. Never has. I don't really know why." She left the button alone and let her fingers trail down his firm abdominals to grip his silver belt buckle. His stomach contracted at her touch and since her urge was to shove her hands into his pants, she decided to let go of him and back the Hell up.

He looked disappointed.

"Anyhow, I could hear them from my room last night. He told her about how awful my attitude is and how the customers complain. She told him he should be more proactive about handling it."

"Wow." He trailed the pad of his thumb along the edge of her jaw and angled her chin up.

"I'm sorry."

She closed her eyes and allowed one sweet, sensual peck before drawing back from him. "Quit distracting me."

"No. Test drive?" That damned smile again.

"Why don't you take Mike instead?"

Aaron drew his bottom lip between his teeth and looked off into the distance. "I probably should since I need the talk time with the guy, but you're so much prettier. So, no." He pulled her against the front of his body and slid his hands down into the back of her low-rise pants to palm her bottom.

Her breath sped as he kneaded her naked behind and blew into her ear. If he kept it up, she'd be climbing him like a tree and trying to get her legs around his waist.

"Now, why don't you get the keys to that sedan?" he whispered.

She opened her mouth to rebut, but figured it'd be a case of the lady protesting too much. Instead, she stretched up on her tiptoes to offer him her lips.

"You're not going to make me fight for it?" He slid his tongue between her lips and teased its tip around hers.

She answered him by pulling his head down further, tightening her mouth on his, and grinding her belly against his erection.

Well, well, Mr. Owen. One less mystery about you, sir. Hello, there.

He pulled back, wild-eyed and breathless, and removed his hands from her panties to give her a little push toward the front lot. "Evil woman," he mumbled, repositioning his crotch.

"You started it."

He furrowed his brow and crossed his arms over his chest. "And I'll finish it, too."

"Mm hmm," she said, turning on her heel. If she had been intimidated in his presence before, that feeling dissolved the second she realized how sprung the guy was. Poor thing. She winked at him as she rounded the corner.

Mike intercepted her on her way to the trailer. "How's it going?"

What's he mean? What'd he see?

After studying his friendly expression for a moment, she realized he was talking about cars. She fixed her face. "Oh, well, I think Aar . . . Mr. Owen may take three more cars today. We're going to go drive that one with the radiator crack."

"Yeah?" He held the screen door open for her and waited as she climbed the concrete steps. "The one I steered that little old lady away from? I'm getting the keys now so she can try that Miata instead."

Her jaw dropped. "Are you kidding? The pink pu-uh . . . *punk* car we've been sitting on for a year? I thought you were kidding me on Monday when you said you were going to sell it."

He snorted. Everyone on the lot called it the "pink pussy" except Archie. Archie was clueless. "Yep. It works okay, right? It's just not conservative enough for most folks in town. Fortunately for my bottom line, she's lived her entire life being good and conservative and wants to try something new."

"Huh! Well, good for her. I can really get behind a lady with chutzpah."

And she could. So many women curled up and waited for life to end once they passed their primes. If Mandy had her druthers, that wouldn't happen to her.

They walked together to the pegboard in the office.

"Michael, I'm bo-o-o-ored!" Elly called over with a pout. She was flicking through television channels and turning pages of a tabloid magazine simultaneously. Mandy couldn't help but to notice the brat's picture was on a little inset on the cover. She couldn't tell what the story was about from where she stood, but whatever it was, Elly didn't seem too flustered by it.

Is that what it's like being an Owen? Maybe Aaron wasn't exaggerating. But other politicians' kids don't get this kind of showcasing, do they?

How did one research that? Should she consult Google or would *The National Enquirer* be more telling?

"I'm sorry, love," Mike cooed. I'd take you on a test drive with me, but the Miata only has two bucket seats."

Elly stuck out her lips.

Mike returned the sentiment and laughed. "When I get back I'll take you out for some good old Edenton clams for lunch, how's that sound?"

She shrugged. "I can live with that."

Mike and Mandy plucked their respective keys off the pegboard and returned to the lot. Before they parted ways, she grabbed her stepbrother by the crook of his arm and pulled him in for a huddle.

"What's up, Mirandy?"

She lowered her voice to a barely audible level and hissed through clenched teeth. "Aaron offered me a job and I took it."

"Oh?" His cheek twitched and as he narrowed his eyes toward where Aaron stood, his face took on a slightly malevolent glint she didn't understand.

"Mm hmm. We'll talk later," he said, voice flat.

"What's the attitude for?"

"Sorry. I was thinking about something else."

She didn't believe him, but didn't call him on it. Even if she pressed, he wouldn't relent. He was a rock that way. Instead, she gave the hand gripping his cane a squeeze and offered him and pleading grin. "Don't say anything just yet? I have to figure out how I'm going to do this."

He rubbed the auburn stubble on his chin, still staring at Aaron, and nodded. "I won't."

They broke apart, him tending to the elderly widow, Mandy to the man in the mirrored sunglasses.

On the road, after noting the Miata's close tail in the side mirror, she squeezed Aaron's thigh to get his attention. Her gut didn't feel right. It felt like it had all those times in high school she tried sneaking in after curfew. She'd quietly slip inside and up the stairs, only to find her mother standing sentry in front of her bedroom door.

She was too old to be grounded, but she did have a paycheck due. Wouldn't want to compromise that, even if she and Mike *were* generally in cahoots.

"Hey, pull a U-ie in the hospital parking lot and head back down 32. We're going to take the scenic route today."

"Anything you say, sweetheart."

Five minutes later, convinced Mike wasn't suspicious enough to have his customer follow their unprescribed test route, Mandy had Aaron turn off onto an unpaved country road.

"I get the feeling you're familiar with this part of the county," he said when she pointed toward a nearly invisible entrance on a wooded lot they approached.

"Yeah." She sighed and waited as he navigated between two large trees on the tight path. It was so grassy, it was nearly impossible to tell if they were approaching a big ditch or other obstacle, but fortunately the ride was smooth.

"I lived out here for a while when I was little, before Mom met Archie and before my father skipped out. If memory serves me correctly, we were renting from a woman who lives in Montana. When my father left, we moved into an apartment in town." She laughed and undid her seatbelt as they approached the clearing.

"It's private. That must be nice."

"Yeah, you of all people would think so, Mr. Owen."

He shrugged. "Can't help who I am."

"My friend Chelsea and I used to come out here to smoke. You can't get more privacy than here unless you're in a hole in the ground."

Once they'd passed the tunnel of trees, the boarded-up farmhouse flanked by its empty outbuildings, and what had once been a garden came into view. When Aaron stopped beside the house and pulled on the parking break, she got out and climbed up onto the hood. He joined her, and together they rested their feet on the front bumper while staring at the trees shrouding the road.

He put his arm around her waist and slid her a bit closer so their hips touched. "I didn't take you for a smoker. I assumed that dirty voice of yours came naturally."

She shuddered as he grazed fingertips up the side of her naked right arm.

Focus, girlie. This is a test drive, not a booty call.

"It does," she said, swatting his hand away.

He put it right back, so she gave up.

"Chelsea was the smoker. Or rather, *is*. I tried a couple of times thinking I was doing it wrong, but hated the way it made my fingers and clothes smell. It's hard to get that stink out of silk."

"You wore silk as a teenager?" He slid his hand down her ribs and lifted the hem of her tank, fixing a steady gaze on her as he swirled his fingertips around to her belly.

She held her breath anticipating where he'd put them next, but he froze them just over her waistband—daring her to move. She didn't. "My grandmother is Spanish. Lives in Madrid. She loves buying me the clothes she's not quite courageous enough to wear herself. Her tastes run toward the classics, but every now and then something interesting catches her eye and she buys it to wear vicariously via me."

He gave her an appreciative assessment from the bottom of her bangs down to her feet. "I guess your tastes now are similar."

"I think it'd be accurate to say my taste developed under her influence, so, *yes*." She laughed and laced the fingers of her right hand through the ones he'd pressed against her belly. She hardly noticed what she was doing, and when she tried to undo it, he tightened the weave of their fingers.

She felt the blood suffuse her cheeks and looked away from him. "Um, Abi actually suggested I move to Spain to live with her after Mom married Archie. She can't stand him."

"Abi? Wow, I haven't heard that diminutive since I was in Colombia years ago."

She shrugged. "Couldn't come up with anything better. We went with *abuelita* for a while, but that so didn't fit her. She's got too much spunk, I think."

"I bet, if she's anything like you. Anyhow, I think your grandmother is in good company with the Archie hate. Why didn't you go to her?"

"I don't speak Spanish very well. And it was my freshman year of high school. I thought the culture shock would do me in, but I regret now not being more courageous. Who knows what kind of life I might have if I'd gone?"

"Well, I don't regret it. If you'd gone to Spain and become all civilized, I might never have met you."

She yanked her hand free of his and balled it onto a fist she propped onto her right hip. "Aaron Owen, are you suggesting I'm not civil?" she asked with her eyes narrowed at him.   .

He chuckled and scraped his hair back from his eyes. "Sweetheart, there's nothing civil about the way those thighs of yours look through the slit of a skirt. The fact I can even keep my fingers off the button of your pants right now has more to do with me being crunched for time than proof of my impressive self control." He pressed his lips against the line of her jaw and kissed down the front of her neck to the jut of her collar bone and down even further to the place where her breasts met at the top of her shirt.

"Keep that up and you're going to get yourself in trouble." She laced her fingers through the back of his thick hair and pressed his lips further into her cleavage, shuddering when he lashed out his tongue.

"It's a long drive back to Edenton. I think I can get it together before then."

"How much time do we have?"

He grunted and lifted his face from her breasts to ferret his phone out of the pocket of his slacks. "At the outside, I'd say about forty minutes. Chas and Tina had to make one more trip but I need time to negotiate on the remaining cars."

"And Mike promised to take Elly to lunch so you don't have to worry about her entertainment."

"Yeah?" He pushed one strap of her tank top down her shoulder and covered the exposed skin with kisses. "What did you have in mind?"

"Hmm." She trailed her fingers down the front of his shirt and stopped at his belt buckle. "I probably shouldn't say with you being my boss now."

He grinned. "You're your own boss. We don't even have to work in the same office. Probably best if we're not seen together, anyway. People would make assumptions."

"You mean media people? And why would they if you're not groping me in plain sight?"

"That's what people do. They see a single guy and a gorgeous woman and assume he's trying to bang her."

"And do people make assumptions about you and Eleanor, who's a knock-out, by the way? Or you and Tina, who has a walk that hints she could probably throw a guy's back out?"

"No."

"And why would I be any different?"

He nudged the band of her bra over her breasts and stared at them.

She covered her chest with her arm. "Answer me."

He breathed out an exasperated exhale. "I don't know that it would be. I just know I want you all to myself. Do I really have to justify that, Miranda? It's a pretty base urge. Caveman shit, you familiar with that at all?"

"Yeah, I know a little something about cavemen."

86

She twisted her lips to the right and chewed the inside of her cheek. How was she supposed to feel? Well, aroused, yes, there was that. Okay, a *lot* of that. She could even see working with him and being romantically involved simultaneously, but keeping everything behind closed doors? No public affection whatsoever? That was a tough sell.

It wasn't that she was the gushing, clinging sort of woman at all, but there was a little part of her that liked having a man wrap an arm around her waist possessively when they walked down a street. When she belonged to someone, she wanted people to know it.

The way he looked at her with so much affection after only three days made her curious about his hesitance. Probably wouldn't matter anyway. Just when her relationships started getting serious, the men always made excuses and dumped her. Even when things seemed downright euphoric, out of the blue there'd be some cop-out excuse: "Mandy, I think we need to take some time apart. You deserve better than me and I want you to know that." Or, "I've been considering taking a job on the other coast. It wouldn't be fair to you."

Aaron gave her a nudge. She must have looked catatonic. "Mandy?"

"One month," she said, staring at the road.

"I'm sorry?"

Slowly, she turned her head toward him, managing a weak smile. "Nothing."

No, not nothing! This thing probably has a one-month expiration date. We'll have sex and next month we'll pretend nothing ever happened. Are you okay with that, or are you gonna fall in love this guy who's already said he can't keep you?

He dragged the rough pad of his thumb across her jaw and angled her face up to his. When his lips crushed hers and his tongue lapped her mouth, she forgot what she was philosophizing about. Didn't seem important.

CHAPTER 9

Mandy's fingers felt like satin against Aaron's naked chest as she swirled her fingertips down lower and lower, caressing his skin as the suction of her lips made his nipples harden and pucker. Then she pressed those fabulous breasts with their caramel-colored areola against his belly and pulled his face down into a kiss he gladly returned.

Even holding the semi-nude woman in his arms and forcing his hands between their bodies to unlatch the catch of her jeans, he felt what he was doing was absolutely reprehensible. Her consent, in the greater scheme of things, meant nothing. Had his father not have been sitting on the high throne of the North Carolina executive branch, they probably wouldn't be parked on the second abandoned property in three days hiding out like school kids sneaking off to smoke. She'd be in the front passenger seat of his SUV where he could properly bore her to death about engineering and volunteerism, and maybe afterward they'd go somewhere small and quiet for dinner to eat a meal without some stranger engaging him in debate about his father's policies. He didn't give a shit about his father's policies.

She needed a man that could put her up on a pedestal, not one he'd hide behind a computer and a firewall and keep out of public sight. But what choice did he have? If Rick ever caught wind of this new woman in his life, the man would have her entire life analyzed and laid bare before his father who'd make the ultimate judgment: "Dump her. It's bad for the campaign." He was prepared to do no such thing.

She broke her lock of his lips and slid off the hood of the car, beckoning him to follow with a cheeky grin. When the soles of his brogues touched the ground, her nimble fingers were already at his belt buckle, loosening the strap and then pulling it free. She unbuttoned his pants, unzipped them, and helped them down past the erection tenting his boxer briefs.

She danced her fingers lightly over the silky hair at his waistband then plunged her hands into his shorts without further prelude.

He sucked in a breath and held it as her fingers tightened around his aching hard cock.

She extracted one hand and used it to nudge his elastic waistband past his hips and down to join his pants around his ankles. The edges of her lips quirked up into a smile, then he was in her warm mouth and nearly down her throat.

"Oh, shit."

For a moment he was unsure of what to do with his hands. Usually, he'd have absolutely no compunction about grabbing the back of a woman's head and demonstrating how exactly he liked it. Those women hadn't had Mandy's class, which admittedly was probably the wrong noun to be thinking about while her lips were around his shaft. He ended up grabbing his own hair at the back, and praying to the god of debauchery it'd still be there by the time she was done. Fortunately, that didn't seem like it would be a long time off.

He watched the gentle sway of her soft breasts as she worked, admired the gloss of her dark hair brushing against the front of his thighs, and felt the warmth of her hands as she cupped his scrotum and applied friction to the base of his cock.

"I feel like this . . . is really . . . one-sided." He gasped; looking up into the clear blue sky and trying quell his need for immediate release. "I think I still . . . owe you . . . from yesterday."

She skimmed her teeth gently against the top of his shaft and backed up just enough to say, "I'll make you pay up" and then she went back to work.

It sounded something like a threat to him, but one he'd gladly stay up all night to receive the follow-up to. He wondered what he had done right in life to have literally stumbled into the woman bowed in front of him. It must have been something pretty damn good.

Finally, he did grab her hair, but not to guide himself deeper into her mouth, but instead to do the opposite. He held her back and removed his cock from her mouth right before he fertilized the ground.

He stood there against the car for a long moment, panting and staring at the little vixen in front of him who'd merely wiped the moisture from her lips, pushed her bangs away from her eyes, and stood back to watch him catch his breath.

He didn't know what to say. "Thank you?" "That was great?" Neither seemed appropriate. Fortunately she was all about business and let him off the hook.

"We should get back. You have a lot of paperwork to do, and I'm sure Archie is wondering what could possibly be taking so long for a test drive."

"Yeah." He kept his eyes on as he dressed, mumbling an oath when she fastened her bra. He wanted to see the full package, all at once. But, that would have to wait until the next time. The next time he needed to hide her away.

*

Mandy waited patiently as the Cars to Work crew efficiently purchased three more vehicles at AA1A. Two they parked to deliver later. The third, the one with the radiator damage, Frank hitched to the back of his tow truck. When Archie asked him where he was going, Frank succinctly handed Archie his notice, gave him a mock salute, and said, "See you, sucker." He would drive it back to Durham for Aaron and Eleanor to deal with later.

"I guess you don't want that last check, huh?" Archie shouted while chasing after the vehicles—quite a feat for his unexercised self. Before he could stroke out from the exertion, Frank stopped at the shoulder, rolled down the passenger side window of the truck and shouted, "Oh, you're going to pay me. You owe me months of pay for miles and gas I put on my truck. You don't want me to sue, Archie."

Mike walked up to stand between Aaron and Mandy and whistled low. "Well, that's embarrassing."

Aaron shrugged. "Hey, offer still stands for that procurement position. Let me know. I'll hold it open for a while. I don't know anyone better suited for the gig, and that's not because I haven't been looking."

Mike didn't look convinced. "Yeah, thanks."

Without another word to Mandy, Aaron gathered up his crew and loaded the SUV.

She and Mike watched him smile knavishly and wave goodbye to Archie as he drove out of the lot, heading north on 32.

"My turn, I guess," she said low.

Mike raised one red eyebrow and crossed his arms over his chest. "You really think now is the best time? I never took you as the sort of girl who had a death wish. Where'd your sense of self-preservation go?"

She gave him a playful punch in the shoulder. "It's still there, but my sense of pride is just floating a little higher right now."

He grimaced. "Well, how 'bout later at home? Might be less traumatizing for the rest of the staff if we keep Dad's tantrum confined to the manse."

His expression alone was worth a chuckle. "I know, but I'd rather leave business at work and avoid him at home like I always do. I guess I'll be moving out as soon as the archduke writes me my commission check."

He scrunched up his face. "Good luck, honey. You want some back up? I'd hate to see you cut down in the prime of your life."

"No, but maybe keep my car running and the door open for me in case I need to make a quick getaway?"

"I think we're probably overestimating Dad's reaction."

"Really? I think we're underestimating it. I just happen to be in a good mood at the moment."

"Good luck?"

"Hey, Mike? Make that sound less like a question and try again."

He snapped his fingers and gave her the thumbs-up. "Good luck, lady."

"Much better."

She took a deep, centering breath before climbed the concrete block stairs. Good mood or not, she moved slowly as if she were marching up to the gallows. When she pulled open the storm door, she could see her mother in the hospitality lounge organizing snack cakes by expiration date.

Shit. No hope for privacy, huh?

Mandy tried to smooth her face to pleasantness before Mom turned around.

"Hot out there, huh?" Mom commented from the tiered cake stand.

"Yeah, it's pretty toasty." Mandy pushed her bangs back from her sweaty forehead and allowed herself a brief pep talk. *You can do it, girlie. Think about it the money once the transition's over. Haircuts! Manicures!*

She was flying sky high, but then the sound of Archie shuffling paper in the office made her belly flip.

Oy.

She hovered near the door, wringing her hands and chewing on the inside of her cheeks as she summoned up her nerve.

Mom closed the overhead snack cabinet, turned around, and rested her rear against the counter's edge. She laced her fingers together in front of her belly and cocked her head to the side with a wide grin, seemingly oblivious to her daughter's distress. "I'm so proud of you for playing nice these past few days, Miranda. When everyone works together, everyone reaps the benefits. I'm glad you see that now. You could thrive here if you really put the effort into it, huh? Maybe work as hard as you did at Ermine's?"

Mandy stared blankly at her mother and resisted the urge to roll her eyes in the manner she'd witnessed Elly perform. "Yeah, about that . . . "

The sound of plastic being slammed against plastic reverberated through the trailer. Archie had hung up the phone, and being in the office with him at the moment seemed a less uncomfortable thing than enduring her clueless mother's encouragement. Mandy gave Mom a little wave and shuffled to the doorway of Archie's office.

She'd never felt her heart beat so hard before, not even the day of Archie and Mom's wedding when Mandy had talked herself into raising her hand when the priest asked if anyone had objections to the holy union. On that day, she was so scared she'd had to hover around the bathroom until the absolute last moment due to her stomach's persistent lack of cooperation and temporary resistance to TUMS.

The wedding coordinator had grabbed her by the arm and forced her away from her bathroom stall into the line-up in the vestibule. Mandy was maid of honor. She swayed all the way through the ceremony, and as soon as the priest asked, she was so nervous the wrong hand shot into the air, sending her bouquet flying into the pulpit where it disbanded at the feet of the minister.

The wedding coordinator had made Mandy's blundering seem as if she had suffered a seizure and ran up the aisle with a wet cloth in her hand. She forced Mandy down to the carpet to fan her face, dabbed her forehead, then announced in a loud voice: "It's all right folks! I think we need to get some food into her! It's been a big morning for Miranda."

Abi, in the pews, had scoffed loudly at the outsider's assessment then mumbled something in Castilian. Fifteen-year-old Mike, on the groom's side, had chuckled until big brother Donald nudged him in the ribs and told him to "Grow the Hell up." Adriana stood cold and frozen the entire time. Archie growled while turning an unhealthy shade of purple. The coordinator dragged Mandy down the aisle to the vestibule then kept her locked up until she had to stand in the receiving line. It had been a horrible evening, and the end result of the blessed event turned out to be her very first stomach ulcer.

"Hey, Archie, can I talk to you for a minute?"

Archie looked up from the coffee splotch he was dabbing off his short-sleeved white button-up shirt. "About what?"

She wrung her hands. "I'm sure this is rather inopportune timing with you planning the big referral event, but I want to make sure you have plenty of time to make, um . . . " She darted her gaze away from his hard expression and shifted her weight to the other foot. " . . . staffing changes if necessary."

Bullshit.

She was pretty sure she'd heard Archie telling her mother he already had an old feed sales buddy on deck waiting for her spot on the staff. He'd probably already filled out his wage withholding forms and picked a start date.

Archie stopped dabbing and raised one bushy red brow at her. "What kind of staffing changes?"

"Archie, I—"

A bit of movement in her peripheral vision made her turn her head to find Mom standing behind her.

Shit. Great, 'cause I need an audience, right? Well, spit it out, girlie.

"I . . . I quit, Archie."

He acted as if he hadn't heard her, resuming the stippling of his coffee stain further into the weave of his shirt's fabric.

Mom moved into the doorway and gave Mandy a cool look. Mandy tried to ignore the expression of betrayal, because she really didn't understand the origin. After all, who had betrayed whom? Mandy hadn't been the one to marry the Archduke of All Assholes. Hell, she hadn't even been consulted in the matter.

She swallowed hard and turned her focus back to Archie. "Did you . . . did you hear me, Archie?"

"Yeah, I heard you." He turned on his little desk light and aimed it toward the front of his shirt. "When are you going to pay me the rent you owe?"

That question made her take an involuntary step forward. "What rent? What are you talking about?"

"That's right. Rent." He stopped dabbing and stared at her. "You know, for living in my home all these weeks without pitching in? You're twenty-seven. You should pitch in."

She opened her mouth and closed it, shook her head, then scoffed. She leaned over the desk and wagged her index finger at him like a Sunday school teacher who'd caught a child tearing pages out of a hymnal. The fear she'd been feeling had suddenly abated. In its place was mounting rage. Her voice careened to a nearly inaudible pitch.

"What the Hell are you talking about? Rent? There was never a discussion about rent! The agreement was the same as the one you made with Mike. I'd work here at the lot in exchange for moving back into the house."

Archie shrugged, nonplussed. "You should learn to get agreements in writing, Mandy. Just like those cars out there— they all say 'Sold As Is.' No warranties. It covers my ass. Folks can't bring cars back."

"My name is Miranda. And unfortunately—" She whipped her head around to give her mother the scowl she deserved. "Children aren't supposed to come with warranties. Shit happens. Sometimes they need help and they have to move back in with their parents even when it's the last thing on Earth they want to do." She scoffed and threw up her hands. "You know what? In hindsight, maybe the women's shelter in Raleigh would have been a preferable alternative. At least there I would have been treated with some goddamned dignity and not like the gum on the bottom of some fucking pompous blowhard's shoe."

Mom grabbed Mandy by the shoulder. "Miranda!"

Mandy swatted off her hand. "Don't even."

"Whatever," Archie said. He turned off the light and then turned the little desk fan around to blow on the wet spot on his shirt. "Either you pay me rent or I absorb your commissions."

At that, Mandy didn't know how to respond. Aaron had purchased five vehicles and had an eye set on a couple more once he returned from his scheduled training event. She did the math in her head. The going rate for renting out a single bedroom she rarely came out of, having use of the bathroom and kitchen, and a place to park her car was probably worth five hundred bucks a month. She'd been home six weeks. She expected 200 bucks commission off each vehicle.

Not gonna happen, girlie. Look who you're dealing with. He makes the rules and shifts the goalposts. Cut your losses.

She sighed. "My math says you owe me 250 bucks. Pay me."

Archie guffawed. "Aren't you a ballsy little bitch?"

"Okay, Archie, too much," Mom piped in.

When Mandy looked at her, she was still wearing that betrayed expression and giving her daughter cool eyes. She had her limits, indefinable as they were. She didn't know whose side to take and Mandy hated her for it.

Archie put his hands up, palms out, in a conciliatory gesture meant for his wife. He was kind to her, if not Mandy. He had married way up and everyone knew it.

"Fine." He leaned to the side to wedge his overworked wallet out of the back of his pants. He counted out some bills and slid them across his desktop. When Mandy took a step forward to count it, Archie slapped his hand over the stack.

"When are you moving out?"

She shifted her lips to the left side of her face and chewed what skin was left on the right side of her mouth. Part of her knew she'd be asked to leave, but had for some reason hoped he'd be magnanimous enough to let her stay until that first paycheck from CTW hit her bank account.

Not happenin', girlie.

"As soon as I pack," she said through clenched teeth.

Archie took his hand off the bills.

She snatched them up and stomped out of the office, paying no heed to her mother's muttering under her breath in Spanish. After grabbing her purse and keys from the staff coat closet, she stomped down the stairs.

Mike was talking to a potential customer at the far end of the lot and Mandy decided not to flag him. He'd find out what happened soon enough, so it seemed the least distracting thing to do would be to leave without disturbing him. She threw herself into her coupe and peeled out of the lot so fast her tires squealed.

She drove hard and fast, growling under her breath and pounding the steering wheel, unsure of why she was so damned angry, but knowing she just was. She was at a stoplight almost near the house before she had a chance or the mindset to count her little pay-off. She counted it twice. The jackass had shafted her five bucks.

Hardly seemed worth arguing for, but she'd certainly never forget it.

CHAPTER 10

"What are you thinking about, Aaron? You're being way too quiet."

He helped Tina move the heavy conference table into the large open square configuration. The hotel staff looked on, already bored with the construction activity. They were supposed to be the ones shifting the tables, but Aaron had gotten frustrated explaining the simple geometry to people whose first language obviously wasn't English. Probably not their second language, either, judging by the faces they made when he resorted to making an L7 with his fingers. He'd even drawn them a sketch and returned from his late lunch to find instead of the tables forming a perimeter with an open middle, they'd made one solid square. What was he even supposed to do with that? Use the tables as a stage and do back flips across it?

"Nothing." He assessed the large square that would seat forty of his growing staff then headed to the wall of chairs.

"I don't believe you. Do you believe him, Chas?"

"Nope." Chas picked up a stack of four chairs and shook his head. "He's either plotting someone's demise or thinking about sex."

Tina paused there between the two men, looked from one to the other, and giggled. "I think both!"

Aaron cringed. Of course she was right. Tina knew her boss far too well. When he didn't provide one of his usual quick comebacks, Chas mumbled "Uh huh," and started pushing chairs under tables.

"Well, well." Tina leaned against the square and crossed her arms over the chest of her CTW heather gray polo. She twisted one of her long thin braids around her index finger and plastered on her most know-it-all smirk. "Who are you killing, and who are you banging? Hope it's not the same person, because that's kind of sick even for you."

Aaron turned his back and picked up a stack of six chairs, hardly noticing the weight with all he had swimming through his mind. "The only person I can think of at the moment who requires killin' is Rick."

"Per usual," Chas said.

"Yeah. Per usual. Banging?" Aaron glanced over at the hotel staff. He didn't trust them, even if they were behaving as if it was their first day on the planet. "None of your business."

"Ha!" Tina shrieked and danced in front of him like a mahogany leprechaun.

"Oh, ho, ho!" Chas leaned against the closest table and let a broad smile span his face. Aaron pretended not to see it. He just kept right on shoving chairs against the square's four sides.

"Chas, I do believe our man of mystery is being more coy than usual which probably means there's a real woman involved in this scheme. Isn't that right, Aaron?"

Aaron disregarded the question and whistled some old jazz standard.

"Anyone I know?" Chas asked, sidling up to his life-long friend. "Is it one of the Richardson sisters? You know, Veronica has been ogling you for at least the past eight years."

As interesting as that revelation was to Aaron, he didn't want to answer. Chas was a talented young attorney and was better than anyone Aaron knew at taking circuitous routes to have his questions answered. If he replied in the negative, he'd just keep on asking seemingly irrelevant questions until he uncovered a clue. The best thing Aaron could do was zip his lips.

"Is there anything I can do to help?"

Aaron thought he must have been imagining things.

They all turned in the direction of the husky voice any lounge singer worth her stage name would have given up a lung to possess. It took every ounce of fortitude Aaron had to not run to the owner of the sexy alto and wrap his arms around her. He stood firm, cutting his gaze left to Tina and right to Chas, who were both walking toward the newcomer.

Aaron didn't like the expression on his best friend's face. He'd seen that look numerous times before. It was his *conquest forthcoming!* face and it was almost enough to set him into action. He pulled his pen out of his shirt pocket and squeezed it hard to fortify himself before following his staff.

Tina was first to greet her. "Hey, Mandy. You took the job? Good for you! We've got to get you a phone and computer and stuff so you can dive right in tonight."

"I'll take care of it." Aaron shouldered his way into the clump somewhat rudely and tried to keep expression off his face. Chas would be all over any emotion he showed and would pick it apart like some kind of preppy psychic.

"Can you two finish up in here?" Aaron dropped his pen into his shirt pocket and rolled back his to expose the face of his gold watch. "We've got about two hours before the welcome session. I want to get her up to speed—let her know who she'll be meeting tonight."

Chas shrugged.

Tina narrowed her eyes at him. "I'm normally the one who does all the up-to-speeding. Are you setting me up for the okie-doke? You aiming to fire me?"

Aaron laughed. "No, Tina. I'm simply letting you get back to doing the job you were hired to do. Haven't you been bitching about that? Besides, Mandy's going to be the lady between you and me. Training should probably come from the top."

"Yeah, yeah." Tina rolled her dark almond-shaped eyes and walked away singing toward the boxes of training materials stacked near the partitions. Chas followed and returned to chair dissemination.

Aaron gave Mandy the blankest look he could manage. "If you'll follow me, please?"

The corners of that succulent mouth of hers twitched. "Certainly. Are you leading me to my computer and cell phone?"

He started walking. "Yeah. They're in your room."

"I don't have a room yet."

"Yeah, you do."

When they were alone in the deserted hallway, he added, "Your room overlaps mine. It's like magic."

*

They hardly made it into Aaron's hotel room before his hands were at the bottom of Mandy's tank, peeling it over her head to reveal her lacy bra for the second time in a day.

"I didn't expect you today," he said, his hands already on the buttons of the jeans he wanted off her immediately. She was playing along nicely and was already pulling his belt through the loops and shoving his pants down his hips.

"Archie and I had a little chat." She kicked off her shoes and stepped out of her jeans as his hands seemed to be everywhere on her all at once. Her waist. Ass. Spine. The crook of her neck.

"Good chat or bad chat?" His shirt buttons popped free with her brazen yank, revealing his rock-hard abdominals and tight pecs. She allowed herself one scant moment of indulgence and flicked at his nipple with the tip of her tongue.

"Bad chat. I quit, and he kicked me out. I've got 245 smackeroos to my name and nowhere to live."

He kicked his shoes across the room and stepped out of his pants and boxer briefs. Once naked, he seemed very interested in getting her to the same exact place and unlatched her bra in two seconds flat.

"God, you're beautiful. Take those off." He looked down her

nearly see-through panties. She got the hint, and did a slow, seductive wiggle out of them, keeping her eyes locked on his.

He rolled his watch off his wrist and dropped it onto the pile of clothes on the floor.

"Well, you'll stay with me at least for the next couple of days."

"Fine." She felt his hands on her bottom then she was scooped up and her legs wrapped around his waist. "And after that?"

"Don't worry about it. I'll take care of you. I want to take care of you."

And she believed him. Maybe it had something to do with the way he pressed her against the wall with her hands bound over her head, her wrists pinned by his large palm. Or maybe it was his cock at her entrance, teasing and stimulating her clit as his mouth seized upon her lobes and neck, then her mouth.

The light growth of hair on his face tickled and made her let out a soft giggle. "You know, I like horizontal sex every now and then."

"You look like a scratcher. The last thing I need is to open up a training session tonight with bloody scratches sticking to the back of my shirt."

"Aren't you a cocky so-and-so?"

Apparently he was. Without further preempting, he pushed his thick cock just past her tight entrance and stifled her moan by putting his mouth over hers. He held her there, very still for just a few seconds to give her muscles time to adjust to his size, and pulled out almost completely, only to sheath himself almost to the hilt.

Pinned there against the wall, she felt completely useless without the use of her hands and inability to work her hips. He was holding her absolutely still, gliding in and out of her, squeezing her ass with the hand holding her up and pressing her tongue into submission with his. With every stroke, he ground the front of his body against her aching clit, making her toes curl and muscles clench around him.

The way she saw it, there was nothing to do for it but go along for the ride. To not try to take control for once. She closed her eyes and cleared her thoughts of everything that didn't matter. The car lot didn't matter. Her homelessness didn't matter. The illicit nature of what she was doing with the governor's son didn't matter. All that mattered was feeling so full and having her body wanted by someone so much for the first time in . . . well, she'd lost track.

"Aaron—"

"Yeah, me too."

He pulled his tongue back from her mouth before she bucked between him and the wall with her orgasm. She might have taken it off with the force of her clamping teeth. Instead, she bit down into a bit of shoulder. It was all she could reach. He didn't seem to mind. He was too busy relocating her to the bed where he laid her flat and pulled out in time to spill his seed all over her belly.

He lay there panting, staring at the ceiling while he caught his breath.

"Bad timing, sweetheart, and I know it. Are you on anything? Birth control, I mean."

She felt like her stomach turned inside out at the ramifications of the question. She'd been so hot for him and eager for his sex she hadn't even bothered to consider safety concerned. It was unlike her. Condom-less sex was usually a deal-killer for her. Always had been.

"I have an IUD. Doesn't protect me from cooties, though."

He chuckled and sat up to hang his legs over the edge of the bed. He walked into the bathroom, ran water, and came back moments later with a damp washcloth.

She took it and wiped her belly clean. "What's so funny?"

"Nothing. It's been a long time since a girl has accused me of having cooties. I'm thinking second grade. It was funny then, too."

"Call them what you want, but I'm serious. I don't know how much you get around, no matter what you claim. You're a goddamned public figure. For all I know you could have multiple baby mommas paid off very handsomely to stay quiet."

He let that movie-star grin span his face then disappeared into the bathroom.

She heard the sound of water drumming against the shower floor, and when he returned, he leaned against the wall beside the bed and crossed his arms over his chest.

Jesus.

She had to turn away from him. His cock was at half-staff as if he was ready to go at it again, and those thighs and calves were just as magnificent out of clothes as she'd imagined. Muscular and sinewy with just the right amount of tan.

"No, no, sweetheart. I leave the carousing to Elly. I'm clean, but you don't have to believe me. Have any allergies I should know about? Latex? I'll sneak out during the mixer later and pick up a bucket of prophylaxes if it'll make you feel better."

"What makes you think we're doing this again, you smug bastard?"

He shrugged then leaned over the bed to pluck one of her traitorous perked nipples.

"Fine."

"Hate to make you put wet panties back on, but without your luggage I don't see where you have much choice. Shower with me? Then I'll drape you in the finest heather gray staff polo shirt available in a unisex size medium."

"What girl could refuse an offer like that?"

"Oh, I have better offers saved up for later." He scooped her up by the bottom and pressed her front against his.

She wrapped her legs around his waist and let him carry her to the bathroom.

*

Mandy was hard to ignore, sitting there in the square between Frank, who'd arrived last-minute right before opening, and Chas who kept nudging her with his elbow and leaning in to whisper who-knows-what. If he kept it up, Aaron was going to have a little chat with him about employee fraternization. It was a total "Do as I say, not as I do" situation and it probably wasn't fair since Aaron hadn't made a public claim of the woman, but still—she was his.

Nothing to do for it at the moment. Everyone, except Chas that is, was looking at him, waiting for him to start.

"It's great to see all of you here in one place. Some of you I see almost daily. Some, I see every few weeks. Some of you I haven't seen since I hired you."

A chorus of chuckles.

"What we're going to do over the next three days is redefine how Cars to Work does business. At the rate we're growing, organizational changes are going to happen frequently. This staff will probably double in size in the next year. Those of you who have been with me since day one . . . "

He rested a hand on Tina's shoulder.

" . . . may find yourselves elevated to leadership positions over the next few months. We're changing the way we procure cars. We're working on building a sort of closet, as it were, of vehicles we can reach into and distribute from rather than scrambling to acquire after the fact based on needs."

He walked to the laptop connected to the projector and activated a slideshow. "We're changing our eligibility guidelines, our screening procedures, and our delivery timetables. We're bringing on more certified mechanics and salvage experts so we can scoop up those well-loved vehicles that need a little TLC. I've got finance people here we didn't have last year."

He nodded toward a cluster of new hires seated closest to the front of the room.

"We gave away a lot of free cars last year. Going forward, we're opening up our program to people who can pay a little. That's where our finance crew comes in. Now, as you all know, I've had some trouble in the past keeping up with the staff. I've double-booked a lot of you on numerous occasions, sending you out to two different client locations on different ends of the state at the same time. I'm not very organized."

Someone, probably Tina judging by the sucked teeth, mumbled, "That's for sure."

He chose not to respond knowing full well Tina's next trick would be her rolling her eyes. He didn't want her to lose a contact lens.

"That's why I've brought someone in to handle all the personnel issues. Make a note in your handbook. Going forward, any issues involving scheduling, PTO, payroll, or equipment should be directed toward Miranda McCarthy instead of me or Tina. Please leave poor Tina alone. She has no idea about your wage withholding. And, in case you haven't met her, Miranda's the tiny brunette enduring our Chas's never-ending chattering."

Mandy smiled and gave everyone a little wave. Winning over the crowd already. He realized the potential.

"She's mean as a snake and full of toxic venom, so don't bug her too much. I hear she bites."

More chuckles from the peanut gallery.

Mandy raised a brow at him.

"Not kidding, she's really vicious. All right, let's plow through this new policy information. I know you're all itching to get to the open bar. That reminds me to make the following admonition. Keep the shenanigans down to a minimum this time and make sure you're parked in your seats right after breakfast tomorrow, because I don't have time to drag a bunch of hungover mechanics out of their rooms." He cut his eyes toward the grease monkey contingency. Eleanor saluted.

Then he got down to it.

Later, he paced in his suite with the door propped open by a box of spare polo shirts while trying to figure out how exactly to deal with his latest disaster.

Elly was sprawled across the chaise in the separate living area, calmly flipping through a magazine as if she wasn't the cause of the day's Owen scandal.

"Really, Elly? Really? What the Hell were you thinking?"

She patted her open mouth as she yawned, then continued turning pages.

"Is this why Aunt Beth is sailing all the way from Bermuda to fetch you?"

"More or less."

"And you couldn't get him to keep his mouth shut?"

She shrugged. "He misses me. It's sweet."

"Sweet?" Aaron's voice was at the point of near hysterics, but he calmed himself down just as one of the new eligibility workers plodded up the hall and bent over the box to seek out size large shirts. When he heard the elevator ding and the doors shut, he took up where he left off.

"There's nothing sweet about him using the British press for a signal boost and telling the world he wants his wife to come home? What the Hell, Elly? Now every person in the globe is going to think Dad is holding you here against your will."

She put her magazine on the coffee table then propped her feet up on the edge. "Isn't he? Him and Rick?"

Aaron covered his face with his hands and groaned. "Do you even love this guy? Just tell me that. Do you, Elly?"

"I'm having his baby, aren't I?"

"Those are two completely disparate issues. Maybe you're not mature enough to realize it. You know, I'm actually quite surprised Dad isn't on the way out here right now to strangle you."

She picked up the remote control and turned up the channel on the pop culture news show she'd tuned into at the exact right time. There was her mug on the screen right next to the Indian ambassador's son.

"Shit. Is it even a legal marriage?"

She shrugged. "Dunno. There were elephants and dancing and stuff. I guess so."

"Oh my God." He laced his fingers through the hair at his temples and pulled. "You're going to screw me six ways to Sunday. You know, I'd planned on having a girlfriend at some point. You're making it hard for me to have a personal life."

She blew out a raspberry and flicked off the television set. "Do what you want. Nothing I do has any bearing on your choices. You can play Boy Scout all you want, but don't blame me for it. Blame Rick. Blame Dad. Blame your own cowardice. Not my problem."

"What kind of woman do you think would have me if she thought her entire life would be laid bare by the media because of her association to me? Huh? Especially with Dad hinting about making a go at the presidency?"

She shrugged again and stood right as Tina came to the door to fetch her for the night.

As a parting blow, Elly added, "Maybe find someone just as squeaky clean as you so when someone gets bored enough to pay you any attention, they won't find anything worth reporting."

Tina rolled her eyes and pulled her away. "Come on, twerp."

That statement stunned Aaron. He actually didn't know if Mandy passed the squeaky clean test. Her background check had revealed no major transgressions beyond the occasional speeding ticket earned in Martin County—which everyone with a driver's license had—but something about the glint in her eyes when she'd had her lips wrapped around his cock warned him she might have needed a bit of taming.

He kicked the box away from the door and headed downstairs to the bar.

CHAPTER 11

"I'm sorry to call you so late, Abi. What is it, three A.M. there?" Mandy watched the bar from her corner booth. None of the CTW staff was paying her any attention there in the dark nook so her whispering was probably unnecessary.

"What happened? Is it Archie? I'll kill him."

Mandy stifled a giggle. "Put your pistol back in the nightstand. Not Archie this time."

Abi sighed on her end. "What's wrong, *abejorro?*"

Mandy chuckled. *Bumblebee.* Abi had started calling her a bumblebee when she was three because she wouldn't sit still during a transatlantic flight. She stared down into her glass of red wine and swirled it while she got her words together. "There's a man I like."

"Oh! Well, he must be some kind of man for you to wake an old lady from her beauty sleep. Rough night. Somebody's dog is out on the terrace barking every time a bus goes by."

"Well . . . yes. It's a complicated situation. His father is a public figure so he makes a point of not dating."

"So he's making an exception?"

"I don't know if I'd call it that. Not an exception and not dating. I think under different circumstances we'd probably hang out for a while before making any moves, but something seems different about him. Well, us, when we're together. It feels right and good and—"

"And super secret."

Mandy sighed. "Yes. That."

"And you like him more than that?"

"Yes."

"I see."

Silence stretched in the distance between Mandy in Suffolk and her grandmother in Madrid. After what seemed like an hour of not talking, Abi dispensed her usual brand of no-nonsense psychiatry in the manner Mandy had become accustomed to.

"Does he like you more than that?"

"Seems like it. But, you know it's always hard for me to read men. I always think I know, then I get dumped."

"Men are stupid. Sometimes women are, too, but I don't count you in that lot. Listen, I'll tell you what I told your mother before she married that American and ran away to the U.S. at seventeen. You want a man who is willing to break some rules to get you. If not, it's too easy for them to let you go."

"That sounds pretty Romeo and Juliet to me. I don't want anyone to end up poisoned or stabbed. I just want to be with a guy I like a lot."

Abi yawned. "You know exactly what I mean."

"I do, but there's another complicating issue."

"What is it?"

"The man is kind of my boss. I got a new job."

"Uh-oh."

"Yeah. See?"

"It doesn't have to be a problem. Your grandfather and I worked together for years and spending that time together in the shop was one of the most fulfilling experiences I've ever had. We learned a lot about each other that way. You'll figure out the boundaries. We always left work at work and kept our personal lives outside of the office. Everything will be fine, *te lo prometo. I promise.* When can I talk to him? See if he's good enough for *mi abejorro?*"

The "him" in question showed up in the doorway of the bar at exactly that moment and was scanning the room.

"Abi, *te adoro,* but just pretend I didn't say anything."

Aaron spotted her there in the corner and started moving toward her direction.

"Remember what I said. Oh! Before I go, I have a big box of clothes to send to you. The girls and I went shopping. They all got you something. Couldn't resist."

Mandy very nearly salivated. She loved those little old ladies so much.

"I'll put it in the post tomorrow."

"Oh, shit, hold off, please. I don't have an address right now. Archie put me out."

"I'll kill him. Come visit? I miss you. *Quiero abrazarte*, eh?"

Mandy's heart warmed at the sentiment. Adriana had never quite been capable of vocalizing her affection for her, although she tried to be generous with her hugs and kisses. To Mandy, there was just something special about being told she was wanted for a hug.

"*Sí, sí.* Ditto, Abi." She ended the call right as Aaron approached and stood a good three feet back from the edge of the table.

He had his hands clasped behind his back and watched the bar via the decorative mirror behind the booth. When he spoke, his voice was low, tone polite and platonic.

"Tired?"

She tucked her phone into her jeans pocket and picked up her wine glass. "Today has been a pretty long day, so yes, I guess."

"Do you have any luggage you need brought in?"

"No. I'm going to go out to my car and stuff some things from my suitcases into a tote. I can carry that myself."

"Okay." He shifted his weight and pulled his lips in between his teeth while he studied her. "Been keeping up with the news down here at the bar?"

"You mean this?" She plucked her phone back out of the pocket and activated its *Daily Mail* app. She held the screen toward him.

He hardly looked at it. His Adam's apple rose and fell as he swallowed hard. He was agitated. Frightened, maybe?

Suddenly, Abi's words about breaking rules rang in her ears. He was terrified, thanks in part to Elly's shenanigans Mandy guessed, and she may have been the only person in the room who knew it.

He cleared his throat. "Your room key should be in your folder. I put it in when everyone stepped out for break."

She tipped her wine glass toward him in acknowledgement. "Busy day tomorrow. I'll probably head up soon to get some sleep. Thanks for getting me set up."

"Glad to have you on board, Miranda."

"I know, right? Mandy is so stinkin' cool."

They both startled at the voice. Chas appeared holding a half-drained beer bottle in his hand and slid into the booth mere inches from Mandy's hip. She noted the twitch of Aaron's jaw as Chas sidled in and how Aaron pulled that silver pen out of his pocket to twirl between his fingers. Agitation again. No, jealousy maybe?

"Did you know she got fired from her last job for being short?"

Aaron raised one brow and slid into the bench beside Chas. "Oh?"

"Yeah, yeah! If I were practicing right now I'd totally take the case. You didn't tell him, Mandy?"

She shook her head. It wasn't something she really discussed widely, and had only told Chas because he was discussing tailoring and dry cleaning . . . the *other* thing she thought was a racket.

"Mind if I tell him?"

She blew out a breath. "Be my guest. I guess he'll find out soon enough, anyway."

"Okay, well, the store she worked at made up a new rule that staff could only wear clothing available there for purchase to work. You know—built-in advertising? They don't carry much in the way of petites, so Mandy would have had to have a whole wardrobe full of pants and skirts altered at, what fifteen, twenty bucks a pop?"

She drained what was left of her wine and nodded.

"Well, duh, she refused to comply thinking it was an unreasonable expense and just kept wearing her own stuff. Nobody noticed for a while, because who could tell one plain pair of tan slacks or black skirt apart from another, right? Well, some chick from corporate visited during the inventory overhaul and noticed the lining of Mandy's skirt was the wrong color. She could see it through the little slit at the back. She tried to call Mandy out on it there on the sales floor and they got into it. Loudly. Vigorously. The lady might have let that slide, or at least she said, but Mandy's deployment of a couple of f-bombs in front of a vendor tipped the scale. She got her walking papers the next week."

Mandy couldn't be sure, but she thought she saw Aaron breathe a little sigh of relief. *How did he think I got fired? On-the-clock blowjobs?* Oh, she reserved those for *him.*

Aaron reached across the table and gave her resting hand a friendly squeeze. "Fortunately, we're not so hung up on dress codes and colorful language at CTW. Wear what you want. You'll be working from home most of the time, anyway. And I'm sure you'll make appropriate language choices when you have to address the public."

"Of course." She arched her lips into a smile and looked at both men in turn. "Now, if you gentlemen will excuse me, I want to catch up on this policy tome so the next time someone asks me how much notice they need to give for a day off I can give them a legitimate response."

"Okay. Wise. Someone should probably read that thing because I sure haven't," Chas said with a shrug.

Aaron groaned.

Chas drained his beer and grabbed her hand before she could skirt away. "Meet up for breakfast? The last time I stayed here there was an awesome omelet station and the silkiest cheese grits I've ever had. I rarely get a hot breakfast at home. I should probably get a girlfriend who can cook." He wriggled his eyebrows. "Can you cook, Mandy?"

She saw Aaron's jaw clench and gave the back of Chas's hand a pacifying pat.

"Um, I usually work out in mornings. I'll probably grab a muffin and a cup of coffee and bring them into the meeting with me."

Aaron's jaw relaxed.

"Cool." Chas leaned forward to see around Aaron. "I should probably make sure Frank's okay. He was starting to talk to himself when I left him at the bar."

"Should have warned you about that," she said with a cringe while edging out of the booth. She picked up her pile of orientation materials and shifted them to one arm. "He's a paranoid drunk. Always seems to kick in around the third drink. It's why he doesn't drink when he's on tour. He starts yelling at his guitar. Might want to get him to bed."

"Damn, sucks for him." Chas gave Aaron's arm a nudge. "Help me man?"

"Yeah, let's go. I think he's sharing a room with Marty, who if I'm not mistaken is the pile currently sitting with his face down on that table." He bobbed his head in the direction of a slumbering patron nearby. She remembered him from the session earlier. Nice guy. Had seven kids, all under age ten. She figured she would probably get plastered away from home if she had seven kids, too. Still, she'd made a note of it just in case he started missing time from work later. The old managerial compulsion had kicked right back in as if she'd never stopped coordinating staff.

"I need to start hiring people who can handle their liquor. This is Hell on my back," Aaron whined.

"Huh. You do seem to get one in every group of new hires."

"Yeah. Must be something about working with cars. Party animals and gear heads."

*

Mandy managed to transfer her clothes and toiletries from her car to Aaron's suite without being spotted by anyone of consequence, although she did have quite a fright when someone knocked on the door. She automatically put her hand on the lever to pull it, then remembered at the last possible moment it wasn't her room. Common sense kicked in, so she pushed a chair over, climbed up on her knees, and squinted through the peephole. Turned out to be a hotel staff member holding a clipboard, and since Mandy couldn't imagine what she wanted at that late hour, she waited until the woman walked away. When she was gone, Mandy quickly and quietly opened the door and placed the *Do Not Disturb* tag on the lever. The woman had left behind a survey about the conference room set-up.

Aaron slipped in about half an hour later with an expression of absolute exasperation of his face.

"Jesus Christ, Chas wanted to talk me to death about tort reform and tried to come up to the suite." He flopped onto the bed facedown and heeled off his shoes without looking. She adjusted her heavy black gasses on her nose and capped the highlighter marker she'd been using to draw attention to important staff traffic issues. If he had noticed her sky blue sheep pajamas or her dorky glasses, he certainly didn't seem to mind.

"How'd you get rid of him?"

"I told him I was expecting a phone call from my father about the Elly scandal, and I guess he didn't want to be in the room when it occurred."

"Is he typically present during Elly fallout events?"

"More often than not, it seems." He rolled over and pushed himself up onto his elbow, then stared at her, his shock registering in how he eyed her from head to toe. "But Elly is always in some sort of trouble." He made a *come here* gesture with his hands, so

Mandy put down her manual and crawled onto the bed.

"When'd it all start?"

He sat up and started fiddling with the buttons of his polo shirt. "Hmm. Hard to pinpoint. She's always been a bit off the rails, but I'd say she really started grabbing for attention right around the time Dad became North Carolina's secretary of state." He pulled the shirt over his head and let it fall to the floor.

"You're going to have to help me out here. I don't keep up with any offices beyond governor and lieutenant governor. Sorry." She shrugged. If he wanted a girl interested in politics, he'd picked the wrong one. She watched his face carefully for signs of revulsion, but he only bent forward to peel off his socks.

"About eleven years ago, I think, so Elly would've been twelve. She went through a lot of private schools that year. Got brought home by the cops a few times. That sort of thing." He unbuttoned his slacks and shimmied out of them, letting them fall to the floor, too.

"You mind taking those off?" He pointed to Mandy's pajamas before sandwiching himself between the covers.

"Not sexy enough for you?"

"Not by half. I forgot you were a UNC grad. If I'd known you have so much team spirit, I might have had second thoughts about hiring you. I get enough of that March Madness rivalry shit in the office as it is." He tapped the bedside lamp off and reached for the remote control.

Mandy spread on the evilest smile she could manage. "You went to State, didn't you?"

He turned off the television so the only light remaining was from the hallway in front of the bathroom. "Yeah. I'll get you a cute little nightie with State wolves printed on the fabric. I think that's more your speed."

"Whatever!" She got under the covers, sheepy pajamas and all.

"Oh, you thought I was kidding?" He sat up and straddled

116

her waist, pinning her wrists over her head once again while he unfastened the buttons of her top.

"Learn to love the sheep, baby. The sky is blue because the Lord loves the Tar Heels."

"If you're going to sleep in my bed, you'll wear red." He pulled her top off her arms and tossed it toward the nearest trash receptacle. "Or nothing."

Before she could balk, the sensation of his warm tongue on her nipple stilled her words. And just like that, a little light bantering and close proximity and he was hard as a rock against her thighs.

"*Nothing* sounds okay. We can make the bed neutral territory."

"Mm hmm." He kissed down, down, down to her naval, made a slow, circuitous lick around her bellybutton then kissed some more until he was at the waistband of her shameful pants. There, he paused to hook his fingers beneath the elastic and drew her pants and panties down in one easy glide, stopping when he reached her ankles.

She kicked them off the end of the bed and felt his fingers glide up her legs from feet to knees then stopping at her thighs. He nudged them apart a bit, and then more, and then more still so she was fully exposed and feeling rather brazen with the cool breeze of the air conditioner fanning down on her from the vent.

"I owe you this," he said, parting her sex with his fingers and bending his face over her thighs.

She considered any number of snappy retorts, but in the end decided to keep her mouth shut for once. Having the last word wasn't worth experiencing the delay of his skillful tongue against her most delicate area. Instead, she just relaxed against the pillow and let him hold her thighs down against the mattress as he probed inside her with his tongue and sucked at her aroused clit with those soft lips.

She squashed her compulsion to tell him to use fingers there or to rub that, and instead let him do it his way. His way was just fine, and although she ached for his cock to fill her once again, his careful, considerate attention to her sex was more than adequate. She laced her fingers through the back of his thick hair, encouraging him, creating more friction from his stubble against her sensitive folds. When she was close, he worked in one finger, then two, and flicked them against her belly.

He was right. She was a scratcher. At least the cuts on his shoulders would have overnight to scab.

*

The next two days of meetings were seamless and informative, thanks to Aaron's charismatic leadership and the support of his long-time crew who not only took their jobs quite seriously, but also had become something like ambassadors for the cause. He was proud of every single one of them as he made the rounds and watched them participate in breakout sessions and brainstorming clusters.

Mandy had fit right in where he expected, and already had Tina and Eleanor trapped in her orbit. She was a quick study, and by Sunday morning at the closing breakfast already had the new staff tracking system up and running. She'd spent most of her nights working on it on her new laptop, in fact. He had to drag her to bed. He was lonely.

Already, he'd grown used to waking up in a sweaty tangle of limbs with the petite hotblood. He loved opening his eyes to find her body curled into his, her long bangs covering her face, lips slightly parted. He loved having her sit there on the edge of the bed watching him pull on his socks and shoes. He loved how when she counseled Elly, rather than stomp and huff away, Elly would sit thoughtfully a while and just think. He loved how comfortable she was at her most casual—sprawled on the sofa in the living area in those damned awful pajamas and in her glasses, holding the television clicker, and laughing unabashedly at the corniest jokes late night television had to offer.

He didn't get it. There was a rightness about her proximity—her presence in his life—that seemed prescribed. She fit into a space he hadn't even realized was empty without even pursuing him. She hadn't pursued him like all the other girls did. Maybe that was it?

Well, he may not have understood the phenomenon, but he wasn't ready to strain its limits just yet. Eleanor had offered to put her up once learning of her housing situation, but he'd stepped in and informed his mechanic Mandy had already made arrangements. He sent her to his apartment in Durham with the spare key, urging her to make herself at home.

Meanwhile, he headed south along the coast toward Southport with Elly in the front seat of his SUV. They were due to meet their aunt, who'd keep Elly at her cottage there until she got her travel documents re-issued. Then she'd hide her out in Bermuda until Carter could whisk the maternal waif away.

Aaron was quieter than usual, because even self-centered Elly noticed his brooding.

"You're awful quiet, big brother. What's wrong? Chas keep you up all night?"

He said nothing. He extracted his pen from the pouch of the driver's side door and twirled it in his left hand.

"Okay. Maybe you'd like me to guess. Is that the game we're playing?"

"I'm not playing any games, Elly."

"Then what is it? Normally, you'd be using this time to lecture me without letting me get a word in edgewise."

"You want a lecture? I have one or two rehearsed."

"Not particularly, but if it's on the horizon, I'd just as soon get it over with now rather than later. I'd like to nap."

He tapped his pen against the door's armrest and ground his teeth.

"Is it about work?"

"No."

"Ooh! I like this game. If I ask a direct question you'll answer, right?"

Silence again.

At that, Elly seemed to decide to try another tactic. "Mom's plan was to keep my marriage hidden until after the gubernatorial election."

"That's more than a year from now."

"I know, but sometimes the public has a long memory."

He dropped his pen into the receptacle and used his freed hand to rub the stubble on his chin. He hadn't shaved it that morning because Mandy said she liked a little scruff. She'd certainly seemed to like the way it felt on her thighs. He shook off the thought. All of his spare thoughts went to Mandy. It was like some kind of sickness, pervading every pore of him.

"Maybe you should explain to me why you're engaging in the practice of covert marriage in the first place, Elly. Getting married in and of itself isn't a particularly scandalous activity. You're a grown woman, even if not a particularly mature one. No one should give two shits about your matrimonial status."

"You really don't know anything about the Patels, do you?"

He shrugged and activated the cruise control. They were finally out of an area where stoplights throttled the trip every two miles. "I don't keep up with the political and diplomatic shit. You know that."

Elly's laugh sounded like a frightened pig's squeal. She'd leaned as far over as she could beneath the seatbelt and nearly lost her breath from the uncontrollable giggles. "Fine governor's kids we make!" she said when she finally caught her breath.

He managed a chuckle. Maybe it was a little bit funny. His voter registration card still listed him as unaffiliated. Obviously the press hadn't caught wind of that particular snub yet. His own father didn't know. His mother did. Some campaign literature from the other side was sent to the house one year and she called him on it. He'd had to explain he was getting junk mail from both sides *and* the independent guy.

Elly twirled a long strand of her hair around two clamped fingers. "Here's the thing. The Patels are sort of well known for their extreme viewpoints about certain issues."

"Issues like what?" He looked over in time to see Elly shrug.

"Well, suffice it to say a few issues in direct opposition to components of Daddy's platform."

"If I didn't know any better, I'd say you intentionally sought this guy out just to ruffle Dad's feathers."

Elly was suddenly very interested in the state of her manicure.

"You did, didn't you?"

Another shrug. "Well maybe at first, but have you seen Carter? Oh my god, he is so yummy."

"Yeah. I've seen him. Not my type. Now that I understand what's going on, I can see why Rick is so disgruntled."

"Are you mad at me?"

"No. In fact, I think it's hilarious. Not the secret baby shit, but the fact Mom tried to keep it a secret from Dad. I didn't think she had it in her."

"Oh, she's full of surprises. Just you wait."

"What do you mean?"

"Nothin'." She flipped her little coin purse in the air and caught it.

The pattern seemed strangely familiar.

CHAPTER 12

Mandy used the reflection of her rearview mirror to tuck her long bangs up into the silk scarf she'd tied around her head a la Audrey Hepburn. In her glove compartment was her second-best pair of sunglasses: the oversized ones with the very dark lenses and tortoiseshell frames she wore only in a pinch because they made her nose disappear. She grabbed them, shoved them onto her face, and adjusted the closure of her wrap dress by securing a brooch where it came together at the bust.

She hadn't actually planned to leave the apartment that day, having an entire stack of reference check calls to make, but while reading the newspaper over Aaron's shoulder at breakfast she saw a sales ad for her old haunt, Ermine's. Ermine's *never* held sales. They hadn't had to. The stock, when she was there, was carefully selected by her experienced co-manager and often exclusive to the store. For instance, Ermine's was the only place in North Carolina that stocked Sweet Louisa leather goods.

She had a turquoise Sweet Louisa wallet, a crocodile-print wristlet, a silver glasses case, *and* a black evening clutch she kept wrapped in tissue paper and planned to dig out of storage very soon. That was in addition to the casual grapey clutch Chelsea kept trying to snatch. Mandy loved the sweet and quirky fabrics used in the linings and how the tags sewn inside always had little compliments like *I love your style!* and *You should be a model.*

For Ermine's to be having a sale, something must have really changed in the three months since she was canned. So, she was there to snoop. She'd waited a good hour until after Aaron left for work to dress and slip out, then drove the twenty minutes to the store hoping the best, but expecting the worst.

The shop windows were dark and devoid of their usually glorious seasonal displays when Mandy walked up. In the past, they had been works of art created by an enthusiastic junior manager who had a background in theater. One year he'd used rolled up shawls and tights as tree ornaments in a Christmas display. The customers, many whom had patronized the store since its opening in 1955, loved and expected the attention to detail.

As Mandy stood in front of the cheerless store, the only things in the windows were heavy black drapes behind four stark white mannequins clad in barely there cocktail dresses she wouldn't be caught dead in. If she had wanted to show off her underwear, there were better ways to do it.

She took a deep breath to gird herself and pulled open the door. After two piddly steps into the formerly grand store, she froze. "What. The. Hell."

The gorgeous hardwoods were gone, replaced with a black polished cement floor. The old wood shelves and stands were gone, too, and in their place were utilitarian metal T-stands chockfull of polyester fashions. Even the smell, formerly rich and slightly sweet smelling from the polish the loving cleaning crew used on the antique accents, was now flat and institutional. Antiseptic, even.

What had once been a store little girls looked forward to growing into for their graduation dresses or first pair of sensible black pumps was now a teenybopper's delight. Her breath caught and she felt tears welling up behind her eyes. Where was the Sweet Louisa? There had formerly been an entire corner devoted to the line. In its place was nylon backpacks and stands filled to the rims with funky canvas shoes.

"Like, can I help you find something?"

Mandy turned around to ogle the source of the voice. She didn't recognize the sales girl nor any of the attire she was clad in. It was cheap. Disposable. Barely covering anything, just like everything else in the store. Being taken over by a corporate conglomerate was the worst thing that could ever happen to Ermines, even if their books were in the black. The charm was gone. Apparently, so was the staff. Her firing suddenly had an extra stink to it, 'cause she damn sure didn't fit in with the new vibe.

"No, thank you," Mandy said, adjusting her scarf. "I don't believe I'll find what I need here."

"Oh, like, do you need a special size or a different color? We can order something for you and have it Thursday morning."

Mandy shook her head. "I don't think so."

The girl shrugged and was turned to walk away, but Mandy's curiosity got the best of her.

"Excuse me, is Taylor working today?"

The girl cocked her head to the side and squinted. "I don't know that name. I've only been here three weeks, though."

"How about Alaina?"

She shook her head. "Nope. Sorry. Don't know that one, either."

"Great. Thanks." Mandy retreated to the door and left without looking back.

She was halfway back to her car and had started unwrapping her scarf when raised voices from the loading dock at the side of the store grabbed her attention. She paused and cocked her head to the side expecting to see the usual white delivery trucks, but her breath caught in her chest when she realized it wasn't one of those. It was the distinctive, paisley-printed delivery truck of Sweet Louisa! She started running. It was as if her feet were moving of their own volition. She didn't stop until she reached the driver who was screaming so loud at the receiving manager—also someone Mandy didn't recognize—the veins in the driver's neck were standing out.

"What's wrong, Toby?"

Toby's eyes went wide as he saw her there and he opened his arms for a hug. "Mandy! How the Hell are you? Where've you been?"

Holley Trent

"I got fired three months ago. I'm just visiting and . . . well, I see everything has changed." She shifted her gaze to the tall, lean manager dressed in faded flare jeans and a cropped summerweight sweater. She pegged her to be around forty and raised a brow at the woman's uneven bottled tan.

"That's probably the best thing for ya. Listen, I'm just trying to pick up the Sweet Louisa stock that got recalled because they don't wanna sell it anymore."

"Huh? Why the Hell not?" Mandy crossed her arms over her chest and glowered at the woman.

The manager shrugged. "It's not hip enough."

Mandy scoffed. "You're fucking insane. Good luck making up that big gaping hole in your profits at quarter's end." She turned back to Toby. "So, what's the problem?"

"They can't find the stock. Or at least they claim. You know how much that stuff is worth?"

Mandy nodded. "I do."

"We're not responsible," the manager said.

"That's what she keeps saying. The big boss is coming out here to deal with it, and let me tell you, she ain't happy about it. She don't come out of her studio too much. Hope she don't have my head for this, but there weren't no one else who could come."

"I'm sure it'll be fine," Mandy said, though she was thinking quite the opposite. What had they done with all that back stock? Liquidated it? If so, they deserved whatever blowback they got. "Good seeing you, Toby. Uh . . . where's the new North Carolina vendor?"

He shrugged. "Still looking. We'll probably just keep the excess at the outlet until the boss vets the boutiques. Oh!" He dug in the pocket of his jumpsuit and handed Mandy a card. "I don't give out too many of those, but you're special."

She studied the paisley-decorated paper and felt her heart go pitter-pat. She imagined there must have been stars in her eyes.

"Thanks, Toby."

"You got it."

Mandy blew him a kiss and continued her trek to her car. As she held her arm up to remote her car locks open, a familiar voice called out to her from across the lot.

"Is that my Mandy Candy?"

She turned around just in time to see Phil Armentrout punched in the upper arm by a pretty redhead.

"Ow!" he whined while rubbing his bicep. He bid the woman to wait by his car while he picked his way across the packed lot to Mandy.

He held his arms out for a hug but she put up her hands to ward him off. "Hi, Phil. Sorry, I'm . . . uh . . . recovering from strep." She coughed twice.

Phil shook his head. "Damn, again? Strep really loves you, huh?"

"Yeah, it does. Let's walk and talk. I have somewhere to be."

She tried to sound pleasant as often as she could, but Phil had been one of those break-ups that had left her feeling cold for a long time afterward. He was the one who said he was seriously considering moving west, but then she saw his car several months later still parked in front of his townhouse. There was no 'for sale' sign in the window, nor was the unit available to rent. She hadn't confronted him about the lie, not even when he'd come into Ermine's with some new woman on his arm—and not the redhead.

"I haven't seen you in a while, hot stuff. Where've you been keeping yourself?"

"I moved back home for a while." She pulled the handle of her door and descended into the driver's seat. "I'm back now."

"Oh yeah? I heard Mikey busted himself up really good." Phil rubbed his chin and leaned against the top of her open door. "He around still?"

"No, he moved home as well."

"Yeah? Hey, you got a card or something? We can meet up for sushi for old time's sake."

"No, sorry. I started a new job recently and don't have cards yet."

Phil stood up straight and started to feel around in his own pockets. "Where ya workin'? Another clothing store? You here to scope out the competition?"

"No, I work with the Cars to Work organization."

Phil froze. "You mean that program headed up by the governor's son?"

"That's the one."

He found a cream-colored card in the rear pocket of his slacks and held it out to her. She palmed it without reading, intending to toss it as soon as she passed a trash receptacle.

"What's that like? He's a mysterious guy, huh?"

She just smiled while she pulled her seatbelt across her body and buckled it. "Mm hmm. I guess he is. We don't work together much, truth be told. He's always traveling and I work from home."

Yeah, Aaron's home.

"Maybe I'll come keep you company some lunchtime, huh?"

Oh, Aaron would just love that.

"Hey, I think your friend is getting impatient." She bobbed her head in the direction of the scowling redhead who'd moved up to the back bumper of Mandy's coupe.

"Send me an e-mail!" Phil said as she pulled the door shut. As she steered out of the lot, she could see the redhead jabbing Phil with her index finger as she yelled. Phil was holding his arms out for a hug.

Right.

*

"Why are you so tense?"

Aaron kneaded the tight knots of Mandy's shoulders as she

bent over her laptop, finalizing staff travel plans for the upcoming week. She could see why he had had so much difficulty keeping track of the team. She'd nearly pulled out a quarter of her hair trying to assign staff to five different assessment outings on the same day. Since most of the staff lived in central North Carolina, it was like a crap shoot as to who'd get sent to some far-flung place. They wanted to keep the budget lean, and tended to avoid sending staff out for overnight outings, but unless they got more hires in the western and far eastern parts of their region they'd have no choice but to require the staff be road warriors.

She rolled her shoulders and moaned when he leaned her head to the side and laid kisses on her neck. "I think I've been sitting in front of this computer for too long."

"Well, I agree. Why don't you take a break?" Aaron pulled Mandy, rolling chair and all, back from the desk and lifted her by her armpits. "Come play with me. I'm feeling kind of neglected, sweetheart."

She laughed and pushed her glasses further up her nose. "Do you want this schedule done or not? I mean, this is what you hired me for." She wrapped her legs around his waist and held on tight as he walked toward the living room.

"Yes, it is, and can I just say you're doing a bang-up job?" He tossed her onto the sofa and straddled her waist before she could sit up. "I like being able to spend more time tinkering with cars. I *don't* like being hundreds of miles away from you when you slap me on the schedule to fill in for Chas when he has to be in court."

"It's your job. Your charity."

"All right, know-it-all." He crushed her mouth with his and kissed her dizzy. "When's the last time you left the apartment anyway?"

When she caught her breath, she swatted him back a few inches and sat up. "God, I don't know. Wasn't I at the office on Tuesday?"

"I don't know. I was in Ferrum on Tuesday."

"Pretty sure it was Tuesday, then. That's the night Carter Patel was on the news again, right?"

He flopped backward against the armrest and rubbed his eyes with the heels of his hands. "Shit."

"I could probably work from the organization office a few days per week. I'm getting a bit stir crazy."

"After this latest stunt? I don't know. I'm being tailed every time I leave the gates here and it'd be sort of questionable having us both in the same complex."

"Since I can't afford to live here alone on my salary, you mean."

"You want a raise?"

"That wasn't my point."

He blew out a breath. "I guess I'll give credit to Carter for figuring out a way to divert attention away from Elly for five minutes even if it makes my life an absolute nightmare."

Carter's maniacal plan had been to plant a seed in the media that Aaron was getting married any day now. His phone wouldn't stop ringing from all the press hounding and the photographers from gossip rags following him around. He'd had to change his work cell phone number and had started leaving for work under cover of night.

She couldn't exactly blame the public for being curious. The young public could give a shit about his politics. They only wanted to know whether he had a girlfriend, and hoped he didn't. Well, he didn't. Not exactly.

She sighed and began chewing on the inside of her left cheek. When he uncovered his eyes, his face fell. He scooped her into his embrace and just held her there.

"Sweetheart, I'm sorry. I know this is hard. You've got probably the worst job in the entire organization and now I've got you trapped here like a hamster in a cage."

"Part of that is my fault. I could find my own apartment. If we kept at least that part of our lives separate—"

"No!" he interjected, holding her back at arm's length to give her a look he hope conveyed his displeasure. He took a deep breath, closed his eyes, and shook his head. "No. I'm sorry, Miranda. I don't mean to snap. You seem to run into an ex every time you leave this place for an errand or to pick up groceries. As long as you're here, I feel like I have a stake on you. I just don't want us going backward."

"Huh?" She arched one brow upward. "And where exactly are we, Aaron?"

His face smoothed to a blank as he stared at some spot on the wall over her head. When he'd found the words, he whispered, "I don't know."

She gave a slight nod and edged back away from him to stand. She returned to her computer and woke it up from snooze before retaking her seat at his oak desk. "Mike sent me an e-mail."

"Oh yeah?" Aaron rubbed his eyes and blew out an exasperated breath. An unsettling knot had formed in his gut and that announcement did nothing to ease it. "What, is he finally refusing my job offer outright?"

"No. He didn't mention the job at all, actually. He said Archie is bellowing about the cars still being stored on the lot and wants to know when they're going to be picked up."

"Shit. Somewhere else I have to be. Is there anyone else who could possibly go? Frank, maybe? He still lives out there, doesn't he?"

She shook her head. "Not a good idea. I'm not sure whether Archie owes Frank money or if Frank owes Archie money for destroying some property."

"For fuck's sake, are you kidding me?"

"Don't worry. I'm sure they'll come to an agreement over it. I think I've cracked the schedule open. I've got someone I can send."

The runt drives me nuts, but she's efficient.

"I owe you the stars, woman."

"Yeah," she said flatly.

CHAPTER 13

"Are you sure this is a good idea?" Chelsea idled with her hand on the door pull as Mandy dug in her purse for keys.

"No, I'm not. But these deliveries are critical. One of the guys receiving one started his job yesterday. He managed to hitch a ride, but I can't help but to feel we dropped the ball there. We're getting more efficient all the time, though."

Mandy's math said driving out to make the deliveries herself was far more economical than continuing to pay Archie's mounting storage fees. A dumb-dumb could do that math. Chelsea agreed to help because Mandy had bribed her with her favorite Sweet Louisa purse.

Chelsea yawned and checked her watch. She was on her lunch break from the social services agency where she worked. As she was on intake that day, someone would certainly notice if she was missing for too long. She hadn't even signed out.

"I'm really intrigued. It sounds like such a fun place to work. Think there's a place for me in the organization?"

Mandy raised a brow. "I didn't know you were looking."

"Well, I wasn't, really, but I love traveling across the state. Maybe you can post me out on the Outer Banks. I could get some sun while I help the ragged poor."

"You are such a generous soul, Chelsea."

"I know! I keep telling people that. No one seems to believe me, even with the work I do. Maybe it's because I'm pretty."

Mandy let out a sigh and pushed her door open right as Mike limped down the trailer's stairs. He waved and smiled that hundred-watt grin as he approached. When he was close, he drew her into a hug.

"Hey, Mirandy. How've ya been? Missed you." He squeezed her tight and chafed the back of her fresh-from-Spain blouse with his hands as they embraced.

"Great, actually. My stress level has gone down about a million ticks."

"Funny how being away from Dad will do that for ya." He watched Chelsea heaving herself out from Mandy's low car and waved.

"So, where are you living now? You still in temporary housing or did you find an apartment and stuff?"

The trio walked toward the first of the two cars.

"Yeah, I, uh . . . I found someplace to live."

"When are you going to invite me over? I miss shooting the shit with you. What have you been up to?"

"Um . . ."

Chelsea tapped Mike's shoulder.

Mandy whistled low. She was off the hook for the moment. Mike being Mike, he'd probably forget what he'd asked her by the time Chelsea was done.

"Mike, was that you I saw zipping north on 32 on a motorcycle yesterday? I thought you had sworn off things with two wheels."

He chuckled and leaned his butt against the sedan. "Yeah, that was probably me. White helmet?"

She nodded.

"Friend came out to check on my recovery since no one on the circuit had heard from me in a while. I couldn't resist taking his new bike for a spin. Kinda makes me want to get back on one."

"You mean motocross again?" Mandy hoped her furrowed brow was a strong enough signal of her dismay. Never had been before, though. Didn't stop her from trying. "You're still broken from the last time, or have you forgotten already what that limp came from?"

He shrugged. "I know, Mirandy. Still, I've been on bikes for ten years. I can't just turn off the switch and not want to ride anymore." He shrugged. "It's ingrained in me."

"You can ride without competing."

"Whoa!" Mike put his hands up in a gesture of faux defeat. "I'm pretty sure my mother has blonde hair."

"Really goddamn funny, you sadistic jackass."

Mike snapped his fingers. "Damn it. Bet expired, didn't it?"

"Well, fuck, it fucking did, fucker," she sang.

"You've been cursing up a blue streak, haven't you?"

She smiled. "Why don't you ride along with us? Chelsea can follow in my car and that way we can caravan instead of making two trips here."

"Shit, I wish I could help. The only reason I'm standing here in your glowing majesty is because the Archduke took the new hire to lunch."

"That cheap bastard buying lunch? The same guy who wouldn't spend money on a new mailbox even after USPS threatened to stop delivering?"

"Yeah. That one. He'll be back any minute. It'll probably be good if you're not here when they arrive. He's still on the warpath about Frank getting headhunted. You he didn't even care about."

"Well, that makes a gal feel swell."

"Just telling it like it is, Mirandy. If I were Aaron, I'd send one of his guys out to look over the cars before the clients drive them off to anywhere. I know Dad's lazy as shit, but he's spiteful."

"What exactly are you suggesting, Michael Leonard?" Chelsea had stopped petting her new purse and narrowed her eyes at Mike. "Do you really believe Archie would do something to the cars?"

He put up his hands. "Look, all I'm saying is you sold a bunch of mid-range cars for barely a hair over *Blue Book* value and he's not getting any advertising kickback for doing it. He was bitching all yesterday to Adriana. Adriana told him perhaps he should do things just for the sake of charity every now and then, and Dad laughed for an hour afterward."

Mandy wrung her hands and stared at the cars. What to do? Deliver the cars without a lookover? See if she could track down one of the Cars to Work technical crew and get them to Chowan County immediately? Assume Archie meant the charity no harm?

She laughed for even *thinking* the last one, then laughed again from nerves. It was an executive decision she wasn't prepared to make. She was *way* out of her league.

"Y'all, excuse me for a second."

She walked to her car and rooted her cell phone out of the center console.

"Hey, sweetheart, where are you?" came Aaron's deep voice through the speaker. "I sent a few instant messages to your computer and you didn't respond. Put up an away message or something, will you? I worry."

"Um, I'm at AA1A. Listen, don't get mad, but we might have a problem."

*

Calling Aaron "angry" would have been an understatement. He wasn't even sure whom to focus his ire upon; he just knew he was pissed. He tried not to take it out on Mandy since she was trying to do her job, and whom else would Mike have confided in like that? He could have had a bunch of cars with his organization's decal on the back that weren't performing up to his standards. The word-of-mouth criticism might have been devastating.

Archie was a crafty bastard; he'd give him that, because Mike had been right. There was something amiss with the vehicles. Fortunately, the problems hadn't been anything Aaron couldn't fix with a quick trip to the auto part store in Edenton. Archie had just made the cars unable to pass inspection, and a bit less safe in the process. So, Aaron bought gas caps, wiper blades and reconnected the car horn wires Archie had yanked out, grumbling all the while.

Once the vehicles were finally delivered, Aaron wiped his hands clean of AA1A except for one last thing. If Archie wanted to dick around, forcing Aaron to bail on a donor meeting he'd had planned for months, Aaron would be a dick, too. He'd make sure he stripped Archie of Mike and any other able-bodied employee willing to jump ship, even if it meant he had to sweeten the pot to a level he wasn't comfortable with. He had an operating budget to mind, after all.

He fumed while he followed Mandy west on 64 toward the Triangle, twirling his pen in his left hand. Then he turned his phone on and called the woman in the car in front of him. Her voice sounded wary when she answered.

"Yes, Aaron?"

"Want to tell me what you were thinking when you decided to pull that little stunt?"

"What are you talking about? It's my family, whether I like them or not. I think it's fine and totally not suspicious if I conduct business there."

"No, I mean you telling me you found someone to pick the cars up when you meant you all along."

"Are we arguing? Is this a professional argument or a relationship argument? Let me know, so I know whether or not it's okay to roll my eyes."

He growled and was very glad he wasn't in arm's reach of the little minx. He could think of at least one salacious way to shut that rude mouth of hers.

"I don't know what kind of argument this is. Hey, can you stay in your lane, please?"

She blew a raspberry on her end, but righted her steering.

"Can you just tell me if you're going to take off like that? When you told me where you were I nearly had a coronary."

135

"Uh, you hired me to keep track of the staff—the staff including me."

"No, you let me worry about you. You worry about the rest of the lot."

There was silence on her end for a moment. He hated he couldn't see her head above the headrest. What was she doing?

"Aaron, that doesn't even make sense. I'm a grown-up. Let me do my job in the way I see fit. If you can't trust me to do that, why'd you hire me?"

He didn't have an answer, so he ended the call. That woman exasperated him like no other. No sooner had he tossed his phone onto the front passenger seat did it ring again. He snatched it up without looking at the display.

"What, Miranda?"

Silence, then: "Who's Miranda?

Shit.

He felt like he'd just gone down a tall drop on a fast rollercoaster from shock. He sucked in a deep breath to calm the butterflies and blew it out. "Someone on my staff who's extremely frustrating," he said finally. "What's up, Rick?"

"Where are you right now? I called your secretary at CTW and she couldn't say for certain."

"Driving into Knightdale. Why?"

"I need you to be in Durham in twenty-five minutes. I've got a press conference scheduled and you need to be front and center."

Aaron pushed his accelerator to the floorboard to catch up to Mandy. When she gave him a curious look he mouthed, "Let me get in front." She cocked her head to the side in a *be my guest* fashion.

"I'm sorry, what press conference? Nobody said anything."

"Shouldn't have. I threw it together this morning."

"What the Hell for? Is this about Dad's campaign? It's a bit early to be hosting the press, don't you think?"

"Yes and no. This is a diversionary tactic. We're putting some heat on you to get it off your sister, the little slut—"

"Hey! Not cool, Rick."

Rick sighed. "Whatever. I figured you'd be on my side, thorn in your side that she is."

"She's my sister. You let me decide whether or not she's thorny."

"If you say so, kid. Just get down to the charity office on the double. The piranhas are already circling."

"Stop with the veiled speech. What the Hell is the press conference about and why do I need to be there?"

"Come on now, Aaron. You're not really this dense. It's not about anything in particular. I told them you have some exciting news about the charity and they all wanted to get their cameras in your face. They're still curious about the wedding, remember? Make sure you smile pretty." Rick hung up.

"Fuck." Aaron pounded the steering wheel and looked up into the rearview mirror to see Mandy following close behind. He didn't know what to do. He wasn't dressed at all for press coverage and he couldn't exactly ignore them by not showing up. He'd have to throw them a bone of some sort if only to maintain the public's goodwill. He rubbed his chin and looked into the rearview mirror again.

"Hmm."

*

"My name is Miranda McCarthy. I'm the staff coordinator here at Cars to Work. Mr. Owen sends his apologies for being unable to be here in person, however I'm fully versed on the organization's progress and can answer any questions in his stead. First, I'd like to thank you all for coming and for your continued interest in our charitable works."

When she got her hands on Aaron Owen again, she'd . . . she'd . . . well, she didn't know what she'd do to him. She just knew he was going to get it good. She sat up a little straighter on the table edge she was perched on and rested her hands daintily on her knees. He had driven home with parting gushing adoration and promises he'd make it up to her later. The way she saw it, he was racking up a Hell of a lot of favors. A little part of her couldn't help but feel like she was being punished for her earlier independence.

She endured the barrage of questions, refusing any that seemed to be fishing for juicy gossip about the governor or his son's marital status, and hustled the bevy of reporters out of the parking lot with the assistance of the small administrative staff. Afterward, she was in the front office pulling some files to take back to Aaron's apartment when she heard the front door whoosh open behind her.

"I'm sorry, we're closed for the afternoon," she said in a tired voice without turning around.

The secretary Jasmine's eyes widened at sight of the visitor.

"What?" Mandy asked, raising a brow.

"I'm going to get some coffee! Want some coffee? I'll get you some." She grabbed her mug by the handle and skedaddled.

Maybe the last thing she needs is more coffee.

Mandy nudged the file drawer closed with her knee and spun around to face a tall, handsome older man with salt and pepper hair. The suit he wore looked more valuable than her car.

"Aaron didn't tell me how charming you are. Well played, my man, holding those cards close to his chest. Miss McCarthy, that was a stroke of genius the way you deflected that question about your employment history. You've got a knack for answering questions without vilifying the other party, even if they deserve it."

She cocked her head to the side and crossed her arms over her breasts. "I'm sorry, who are you?"

He bared his teeth in a smile. It was nowhere near as dazzling as Aaron's or Michael's, but she could see how it could disarm someone. Just not *her.*

"Where are my manners? People usually recognize me because of the company I keep." He put one elegant hand into his inner coat pocket and plucked out a business card.

She squinted down at it. *Rick Bane - Political Strategist/Expert.* She scoffed at the 'Expert' bit and shoved the card into her pants pocket. She didn't understand the purpose of the job. Was he supposed to be an expert of people, of policy, or some combination of both? She didn't like feeling like she was being gamed and being unable to tell what a candidate's exact stance on an issue was.

Ah. So that's what he does for a living. Muddles the issues. Didn't realize that was an actual job.

"What can I do for you Mr. Bane?"

"I was expecting Aaron. When you showed up instead, I stuck around to see what kind of game he was playing, but it seems like he doesn't need my help after all."

"What sort of help do you provide?"

He just winked.

She rolled her eyes, and gave not one fuck if it was rude. He didn't count in her book as far as customer service went.

"So, McCarthy? I bet that makes you Irish."

She tapped the toe of her shoe against the floor and crossed her arms over her chest. "I'm American, born right here in North Carolina. If you want to get technical, however, I have dual citizenship."

"So, Irish and American?"

She shook her head. "What precisely are you fishing for? Sorry to be brusque, Mr. Bane, but I have a lot of paperwork to plow through tonight. Big staff meeting tomorrow. I'm sure you understand."

"You sound mighty productive. Self-starter, are you? Bet you don't need anyone telling you what to do."

"No, I don't."

"I like that. Ever given any thought to working in politics?"

"None. I'm basically apolitical. I can recite the Preamble from memory if you'd like to hear it, though. Learned it from *Schoolhouse Rock*." She started to hum the melody.

"You're funny. Quick on your feet."

"Is that a euphemism for mouthy?"

"You've definitely got the spitfire trait."

"I've been called worse."

Aaron, showered and dressed in dark jeans and a green shirt that made his hazel eyes pop, pulled the door open behind Rick. He gave her a *sorry about that* expression while the older man turned around.

"I'm sorry to leave you on the lurch like that." His voice was absolutely flat as though they hadn't been conspiring only two hours before. "I know it's not in your job description. I'll make sure it doesn't happen again." He turned to Rick. "You can't just be springing this shit on me. I was way out on the coast this morning. What if I couldn't have gotten Miss McCarthy here?"

Rick looked down at his gold watch and huffed. "Water under the bridge. We did what we set out to do. Now, lovely Mandy with the big gray eyes will be all over the five o'clock news, and not the shenanigans of one spoiled pretty little princess."

The corners of Mandy's mouth twitched and she balled her free hand into a fist at her side. How dare he? Who was he to insult that young woman? It was one thing for her or Aaron to give Elly a hard time to her face because they had the best intentions. But this guy? She didn't like him one bit. Still, she held her tongue. Elly was Aaron's sister. It was his fight.

"If you'll excuse me, gentlemen, I'm going to go treat myself to a working dinner."

Rick opened his mouth to say something in response, but before he could spit it out Aaron said, "I'll see you at the meeting in the morning. Can you forward the staffing projections to me beforehand?"

"Certainly."

Before the door swung closed behind her, she heard Rick say, "Well. She's a spunky little thing. Where'd you get her? Thought you liked your help a little more passive."

Asshole.

CHAPTER 14

Mandy squirmed out from under Aaron's heavy arm and reached for the cell phone ringing on the bedside table. She read the time display before answering. One A.M. *Damn it.*

"Hello?"

"That you Mandy?"

"Who the Hell is this?"

The low tenor on the other end chuckled. "Aw, honey, you forgot my voice already? I'm crushed."

"Bo?"

"That's the one, baby. How the Hell are ya? I just got off work or else I wouldn't have called so late."

"Um . . . hi, Bo. Not to be rude, but why are you calling me?"

Aaron stirred. She held very still and hoped she'd end the call before he fully woke. Her ex on the phone at dark o'clock would just be far too awkward a thing to explain, even if she hadn't been the one to initiate the call.

"I heard you moved back to the Triangle."

"Yeah, I did. What of it?"

"It may just make my life a little easier now that . . . *well!* Anyhow, I swung by the car lot today with a pan of spanikopita my mom made for you. You know, she asks about you all the time still? Mike said you quit a couple weeks ago, which was a surprise to me, but then I saw you on the news tonight. Working for Aaron Owen, huh? Damn, girl, you looked good."

"Wait—your mom made me spanikopita? Where is it?"

He laughed. "You always did have a one-track mind. Adriana was in the sales office so I handed it off to her with my regards."

Aaron grabbed the phone with ninja-like stealth. "Good morning, who is this?"

Oh shit.

She couldn't tell what Bo's response was, but Aaron's was pretty telling.

"Yeah, she's in my bed right now. No, don't sweat it, man. Just call when the sun's out next time, okay? Goodbye." He stabbed the end button, held the phone out to her, and flipped his pillow over to the cool side.

"You don't get to do that," she mumbled, slapping his back.

His only response was "mm hmm" before serenading her with his deep, even breaths.

"I'm serious! You can't just go scaring off my friends when they call at inopportune times."

He pushed himself up onto his elbows and gave a tired expression. "Friend, did you say?"

She shrugged. "More or less."

"Right. When's the last time you saw or spoke to this friend?" He sat up completely and let the sheet that'd been covering his chest fall to his waist.

Her gaze trailed down to the bulge it just barely covered.

Get it together, girlie.

She closed her eyes to think about it. Had it been that long ago? She and Bo had started dating just before she got fired and had to move back to Edenton. They dated for about three months before things fell apart on his end. He'd given her some lame-ass excuse about not being able to give her the time she needed because of his long hours at the restaurant. She had thought it seemed like a cop-out because they were seeing each other at least two or three days a week, even when she was in Raleigh and he was in Edenton. The excuse was a bad one and she knew it.

She opened her eyes and found Aaron's expression exactly as perturbed as it had been before. "It's been a little while."

"Your friends always call you at one in the morning?" The dim light in the room made his expression seem unusually dark. "In my circle of friends, the only time we call a woman after midnight is when we're in the mood for a bang."

She gritted her teeth. She and Bo had done their fair share of early morning banging, but she wasn't about to tell Aaron that. "He's a chef. He works weird hours."

"And you work normal ones. Maybe you should turn your phone off after ten."

Her blood felt like it was about to damn near about to boil over. "Or how about if I just change my phone number? That way you won't have to worry about any of my old friends calling me at all. Would that suit you, master?"

He pulled her close to him by the waist and put his lips against her ear. "How would you like it if women were calling me late at night looking for a booty call?"

She shrugged in his arms. "Maybe they do."

"You really think that? We've spent every night together the past few weeks and you still think I'm sniffing around someone else's front door? Un-fucking-believable." He let go of her and crawled to the edge of the king-sized bed where he quickly swung his legs over. He strode in his boxer briefs across the bedroom and snatched his phones up off the dresser. He tossed both onto the bed.

"Here. You can scroll through the history on both. Read my texts. Read my emails, if you want."

She shoved the phones back at him. "I don't need to see that. Besides, you can easily delete conversations and histories with a few easy commands. If you had something to hide, and I'm not saying you do, it'd be the first thing you'd do."

"Jesus, woman!" He raked his hands through his hair and gave it a frustrated tug. "I don't know what to do with you! I never know what's going through that head of yours. I can't get a reading on anything. It's like you're completely passive when it comes to me. You're there, oh boy are you there, when I'm pounding into you. The rest of the time? You're a complete mystery."

That revelation knocked the wind out of her. She leaned against the headboard and stared at her shaking hands. It was obvious to her then that he felt something for her. What wasn't so obvious is what that meant. They pretty much lived together. Even if it had been out of necessity, at least early on, there wasn't anyone she wanted to live with more. She'd never lived with any other man and actually *liked* being a fixture in his home.

What she must certainly did *not* like was the indefinable something they had between them. Was she just a valued employee? A lover? A girlfriend? She didn't like that air of vagueness any more than she liked being hidden away and only trotted out for Cars to Work business. It was all starting to seem so wrong, even though it felt so right. Nothing about her time with Bo, while it lasted, ever felt that way. Although Bo hadn't been nearly as passionate or ambitious as Aaron, when they were out together he liked for everyone to know they were a package deal—an item.

She missed that; that public sense of belonging to someone in the same way they belonged to her. She wanted to stake her public claim on Aaron Owen, and not because she was some gold-digging twat scratching for her fifteen seconds of fame, but because she just liked him that much. More than liked him. Damn it.

"I don't mean to be a mystery," she said, wrapping her arms around her knees and rocking.

"Right." He blew out a deep breath and stalked forward to pick up his phones. He replaced them on the dresser top then pulled the bedroom door open. "I'm sure there's a crime drama marathon on. I doubt I'll be able to get back to sleep, so I'll just let the screen lull me."

She didn't hope for an invitation, and he didn't give her one. He just walked through the door and pulled it shut behind him without another word.

*

Mandy had made a point of taking the furthest seat away from Aaron as she could at the conference table. He figured it was for the best. He was angry and it was probably a good thing there were six staff members between him and her. Especially since she'd worn some kind of gauzy blouse in which every time she leaned over a bit he could see right down into her cleavage. If she'd been any closer, he'd probably try to take her into his office and bend her over the edge of his desk.

He nearly creamed his pants at the thought of pulling her panties down and giving her a well-placed smack on the ass. Hell, the way he saw it, she needed a bit of reining in. Maybe she'd forgotten whose cock filled her so perfectly or whose tongue turned her to jelly when thrust between her legs.

Jesus Christ, pull yourself together.

He took a deep cleansing breath and dismissed the meeting right as Jasmine poked her head into the conference room door.

"Mr. Owen, there's a Michael Leonard here to see you. I sent him to your office to wait."

He saw one of Mandy's eyebrows fly up through her bang, and assumed she was as out of the loop as he about the visit.

"Thanks, Jas."

When he entered his office to find Mike perched on the arm of one of his guest chairs with his cane draped over his lap, he pushed the door shut and strode over to shake his free hand.

"How are you, man?"

"Fine. How's Mandy? It's still weird not talking to her every day." A look Aaron didn't like flitted across Mike's face but quickly dissipated.

"She's good. Adjusting really well. Now, how do I deserve the honor of this impromptu meeting?"

Mike lowered himself carefully into the chair and put his cane on the floor. "Well. I've been giving a lot of thought to your job offer in the past few days—comparing it to the other one I was offered."

"And your assessment?" Aaron opened the mini-fridge stored in the credenza on the back wall and offered Mike a beer. Mike shook his head.

"There are a lot of things about the other job I like. I actually started last week in the evenings. Zipped around from one job to the other while finishing out my two weeks at AA1A."

"Mm hmm."

"It's great. Everything an expert on sports could want in a job."

"But?"

Mike wrung his hands and stared up at the ceiling. "Let's just say I'm young enough to still want to be participating in the sports and not just commentating on them."

"Ah. I see."

And to a degree, Aaron did understand what it must have been like to be on the fringes of something. He felt that way every time Mandy walk outside a door and he wasn't on her arm—an onlooker.

"Do you think you can buy cars with the same éclat with which you sell them?"

Mike shrugged. "Buying, selling. Doesn't matter. It's just two sides of the same coin. Both sides are trying to get their way. I'm just really good at being the one who wins."

Well, fuckin'-A.

Aaron held out his hand. "Welcome to the team."

They shook. If Mike noticed Aaron squeezed his hand harder than necessary in the process, he didn't show it.

*

"Can I help you, Miss McCarthy?"

Mandy had never felt so desperate for shopping therapy as she did right then. And actually having money in her bank account for a change, she figured a nice little trip to the Sweet Louisa outlet would do wonders for her mood. It was at damn near cesspool levels. Even if she did have exes coming out the woodwork trying to mack at her for some odd reason, not a single one of them had that special combination Aaron possessed—the charm, the looks, the sex appeal. She was so sad she'd have to dump him.

"Um . . . " She put down the sunglasses case she was holding and looked up to meet the woman's gaze. How'd she know her name? Oh yes. Press conference. Her picture *had* been printed in the *N&O* with the caption *Miranda McCarthy of Cars to Work discusses hiring push at yesterday's press conference.* "I've already seen all these prints. I guess I was looking for something I may have overlooked before."

The woman tucked a swath of her thick blonde hair behind an ear and let her reading glasses fall down to hang from the chain around her neck. Her smile was warm, welcoming. "Are you a collector? Not too many people know the insider details about when we're open to the public."

"Oh! I forgot about this." Mandy ferreted the open invitation Toby had given her out of her pocket and showed her. "Sorry."

"Ah. Not too many of those floating around. Haven't seen one in about a year."

Mandy studied the card's bent corners from having been stuffed into Toby's pocket for so long. "I used to manage Ermine's before it got bought out by the conglomerate. I got first dibs on a lot of things since I was co-manager. I bought a little bag a few months ago before I left. I gave it to a friend last week and I'd really like to replace it. It was limited edition, so I guess the chances of that are slim to none."

"Approximately. But, just for giggles, which bag was it?"

"Muscadine."

The clerk covered her mouth and had a good laugh. After about fifteen seconds she held up a finger in a *wait* gesture, walked past all the nearly empty shelves and bins, and disappeared behind a curtained door.

Mandy kept browsing while she waited. She picked up a catalog detailing the entire collection since 1987 and coveted some of the quirky vintage designs. The woman came back with a white cloth sack, pushing her glasses back up on her nose.

"Oh yes," she said, looking down at the open catalog. "I wish I had kept a few of those."

"You've been working here that long?"

She smiled and turned to the front of the catalog. There was a picture of one Mary Louise "M.L." Owen, circa 1986, sitting at a drafting table. Mary Louise Owen. The governor's wife. Aaron's mother.

Mandy looked from the catalog, to the clerk, to the catalog once again. "I feel like an idiot. I never made that connection. Sweet Louisa? *Louise.*" She thunked her head with the palm of her hand.

"Most people don't. It's not widely publicized and I stay out of the spotlight. I'm not here much nowadays. I let my little elves run the business." M.L. crossed her arms over her chest and sighed wistfully.

"I guess I know a little something about being an elf. Aaron didn't tell me you worked in fashion."

"Aaron doesn't know."

"How is that possible?"

M.L. shrugged and turned to the next page of the catalogue. "I never lied, it was just sort of a purposeful omission. He probably assumes I spend my days ladling soup at the homeless shelters. I never started this business for the notoriety. The little purses were something I did for fun when Aaron was very young and Charles was working long hours. I grew up around fabric and started with that, then moved on to leather later on. I didn't expect them to become so popular."

"So, you hide what you do from the public? On purpose?" She wrung her hands. If M.L. was in hiding, what hope did *she* have? None. Best to stick to the dumping plan.

"I guess I do. I didn't want anyone to patronize or *not* patronize my business because of my husband's politics. I wanted people to find and buy Sweet Louisa products because they just like them."

"I've loved them since I was fifteen. My grandmother ordered my first one for me." Mandy tapped her chin, wondering what had happened to that little big.

"I'm so glad. Here. Take this with my regards." M.L. extended the cloth-covered clutch to Mandy and Mandy unwrapped it in a hurry.

"It's Muscadine! How do you still have that?"

"I really hate muscadines. Made me hate that bag, too. I signed off on them and then regretted it."

"Are you bullshitting me? If I weren't so sure I needed it, I might have given up one of my kidneys to replace the bag I gave away. I felt like a kid who'd lost her blankie."

M.L. blushed and gave Mandy a light swat on her arm before walking away. "Miss McCarthy, you're so darn cute. I think I love you."

Well, that made *one* Owen. At that moment, Mandy liked the one with the pretty purses a little more than the one whose bed she'd been sharing for the past few weeks, anyway.

CHAPTER 15

Aaron's jean-clad legs were all Mandy could see from her position near Cars to Work's back door. Still, she kept her distance should anyone be watching from the back offices. They'd been very careful about not being found in the same room together alone, and she was about to nip the affair in the bud. No point making it public now. She kept her voice low, knowing sound traveled well from the parking lot.

"Aaron?"

He stopped tinkering and his foot ceased tapping out a beat only known to him. "Miranda? That you, sweetheart?"

"Yes. Mike is finishing up his packing back in Edenton. He called earlier. He asked me if he could crash at my place for a while until he could figure out where he wants to live permanently."

Aaron grunted and slid himself out from under the car on his creeper. He had soot all over his cheeks, his hair was mussed, and brow was furrowed. To her, he looked *wonderful*. She suddenly felt very depressed.

"What'd you tell him?"

"I made up some bullshit lie about the apartment complex needing to move me to another unit because of a flooding issue."

He narrowed his eyes at her as he wiped his hands clean on a rag and sat up. "Did he believe it?"

"I don't know, but either way he's prepared to make other arrangements. I feel like an absolute bitch for not being able to help him out. We've always helped each other."

Aaron shrugged.

"Great." She turned on the heel of her ballet flat and huffed. She had her hand on the door handle and was rearing back to pull the door open when he called her back. His voice was surprisingly gentle.

"Sweetheart, wait. What do you want me to do? Tell me what you want me to do."

It was her turn to shrug. Too little, too late.

"I don't know. Act like you care, I guess? That'd be a good start."

"I do care—don't think for a minute I don't. I'm just not sure how to go about this sort of thing. Secret love affairs aren't described in political handbooks or anything and, if they are, I'm sure they explicitly advise against them. I'm doing the best I can, Miranda."

"So am I. Starting from right now, anyway."

"What's that supposed to mean?"

"I think I need to find my own apartment."

Aaron put his hands on the ground to brace himself to stand and opened his mouth as if to object, but Mandy held up her hand to halt his words.

"Save it. Please, just—just don't."

"No!" He was on his feet and pulled her into the shielded entryway out of view of the windows. He wrapped his arms around her shoulders and held her against his chest. "No. I'll figure something out. You don't have to leave. If you want me to put Michael up somewhere I'll—"

She shook her head slowly and gave his chest a little push. "No. Right now I . . . I need some space. My *own* space. I've gone too long without it and I'm a woman who likes having her own things. I appreciate you taking care of me. I really do, and I know you liked doing it but I just . . . I don't . . . " She shrugged.

His expression darkened and he took a step back from her. "Is it that guy that called you a couple nights ago? That Bo? Or the one whose card I found in the bathroom trashcan?"

She quirked her head to the side and narrowed her eyes at him.

She hadn't thought about Bo for more than five minutes since his call. She'd thought a lot about his mother's spanikopita, but not Bo specifically. Besides, Bo was a nice guy, but compared to Aaron's molten aura, he was a cold fish.

"No, Aaron. I tend to only allow one man at a time to frustrate me. Right now, you're it." She yanked the door open and stomped down the hall, forcing back tears.

After gathering her computer and CTW cell phone, she struck out for that apartment complex she'd seen advertising free cable and half-off security deposits.

*

"How are you doing, kiddo?" Aaron idly flipped through television channels while slouching low on his sofa. The living room was dim, blinds drawn as he sat alone in the quiet with his phone.

"Super. Sick as a dog, but happy. Carter is supposed to be here to get me tomorrow. He's flying in with his family's plane."

"That's great." He turned the television off and tossed the remote. There wasn't anything on worth watching, not that he was able to concentrate, anyway.

"Great? Who am I talking to, here? Is this my big brother or is this a Rick Bane hoax of some sort?"

"It's me, why?"

"Because your usual response would be something along the lines of me wasting my potential and blah, blah, blah, and such and such."

"Oh." The truth was, he hadn't even heard her. He'd turned out after noticing Mandy had left her glasses case on his coffee table. He picked it up and rubbed it between his palms.

"I'm sorry, I was a bit distracted. I wasn't listening."

Elly groaned. "Then why'd you call me?"

He shrugged then realized Elly couldn't see it. "I don't know. It was an automatic reflex or something."

"Okay. What'd Mandy do to you?"

"Huh?" Aaron sat up.

"Don't play dumb. I know you. I may be ditzy, but I'm not blind."

"What?"

"It took me a while to realize it because I'm not so great at putting two and two together when the math is right in front of my face, but give me a night to sleep on it and the answer will come to me in my dreams."

"Elly, does Carter have you hooked on opium or something?"

"Ha. Funny. Look, it wasn't hard to figure out. I realized you like Mandy. A lot, probably."

He struggled to swallow the lump in his throat and when he managed to speak again his voice was hoarse. "Oh yeah? What makes you think that?"

"Dunno. Maybe it wasn't just one thing, but several, but what really tipped me off is that you let her give me advice."

"So?"

"And you don't do that. I don't know if you're aware of it. You've always gotten defensive when people have tried to tell me what to do, or when they've criticized me. You didn't this time. You even left me alone with her, which tells me you not only like her, but you trust her. How many women do you trust that way beyond Mom?"

"I leave you alone with Tina all the time."

"That's different and you know it. Tina's like a nanny or something to me. She's hardass, takes no guff, but she doesn't try to give me life lessons 'cause she doesn't really like me that much."

He raked his free hand through his hair and paced beside his kitchen island, still clutching Mandy's glasses case. He'd seen one like it before, but couldn't put a finger on where.

The spot where Mandy had used to set up her laptop to do reports was still as empty as the day she'd moved out to her own place and looking at it made his stomach drop again. He missed his girl. He missed her clutter and her just taking up space in his life. She'd bundled up her few things a week before and left while he was at CTW fiddling under the hood of some economy class car like an idiot. Mandy had been working at home ever since, avoiding him, though he wasn't sure he could blame her. She *had* said she became easily attached. He couldn't help but to wonder if she was feeling his absence the same way he was feeling hers.

"You still there, Aaron?"

"Yeah."

"I'm right, aren't I? I'm right about something for once?"

"Yeah. I guess you are."

"Hot damn." Elly cackled. "So, what's the problem?"

"The same one as always, Elly. I don't want to have my private life put under a microscope. I want my relationships to work or not work because of my own actions, and not from outside pressures. Neither of us asked to be dragged into the limelight with Dad, but I can prevent making anyone else suffer along with me."

Elly sighed all the way from Southport. "God, Aaron. You're the smartest guy I know. Figure something out and stop torturing that woman. I think mom would like her. She's got class and stuff. I gotta barf, bye." She clicked off and he leaned against the island a while longer with the quiet phone still pressed to his ear.

Class, Elly had said. He stared at the programmed numbers in his phone for a minute, carefully choosing his words, and then dialed his mother's cell phone number.

"Yes?" she answered.

"Are you alone?"

Silence. He heard footsteps then a door being shut.

"I am now."

"I have a problem."

"Legal or business?"

"Neither. Romantic."

Mom sucked in a breath. "Are the marriage rumors true?"

"No."

"I didn't think so. Anyone I know?"

"No."

"Someone at work?"

"Yes."

"So, someone I know. Is it Miss McCarthy?"

"How do you know Miranda?"

"Serendipity is how. I raised you to like women with good taste. Apparently that led her right to me. Do you have a pen?"

He rustled through the mess on top of his desk and found the silver pen he normally kept in his pocket. "Yeah."

"Meet me at this address in . . . oh, twenty minutes? It's near the outlet mall. Try not to get followed. I don't feel like arguing with your father tonight. The only wine left at the mansion is that muscadine swill I have to sample before that festival."

*

"Everything, everything, everything must go! We're expanding our lot and getting ready for the biggest influx of used car inventory Eastern North Carolina has ever seen. We're slashing prices and—"

Mike turned off the television and flicked the remote onto the floor. He put his right arm around Mandy's shoulders and pointed to the screen. "At first I thought Don was kidding me about Dad shooting a commercial, but after having seen it aired seventy-five times in the past four days I'm inclined to believe him."

She crossed her legs at the ankles atop her new coffee table and took a sip of her coffee. She made a gakking noise after realizing once again Michael hadn't put sugar in it. He drank his black and thought she should consider doing the same. She wasn't a connoisseur by any stretch of the imagination. She just poured it down her throat by the decanter-full and hoped she'd live to see 9 p.m.

"What exactly is he playing at? Edenton can't support a used car dealership that size. Most people shop for cars in Hampton Roads or Elizabeth City."

"Yeah, they do, but he's going to be doing something a little shadier."

"You mean shadier than he already does?"

"Well, yeah. He doesn't make much money on the mid-range cars, so he's converting his business model to economy and older model vehicles he can make more profit on."

"How? The profit margin is about the same. Used is used."

Mike shook his head. "Not exactly. Where he's going to make his money is on the financing. He's going to price the cars really low and then screw people on the interest rate. Folks'll end up paying twice what the cars are worth if they don't get repossessed first. Nobody ever reads all the numbers on the financing paperwork. They just read the number telling them what their monthly payment will be and hold out their hands for the keys."

"And he's banking on the fact that people will come from all over to get what they perceive to be a cheap car."

"Yeah. He's kind of subverting the Cars to Work program and other charities like it. People get frustrated by waiting lists, so instead they queue up to have themselves screwed without lube."

"As Abi says: common sense is not common."

"Your nana is smart."

"Yes, she is."

Mandy had actually talked to her grandmother the night before. She'd bitched about her mother's coolness, Ermine's metamorphosis, having her stepbrother as a roommate, and of course about Aaron. Abi had been silent and understanding right up until the last part. When she sighed, Mandy knew she had a lecture on the way. Abi didn't disappoint.

"Listen, *mi abejorro*. People very rarely take the advice of old women on matters of love, but hear this. There was once a woman, not much older than yourself, madly in love with the nephew of the king. It wasn't a one-sided infatuation. He loved her right back. The problem was she was lowborn and there was already a bride chosen for him. Some ugly French woman with a face like a goat. So, he married the French woman."

"Abi!" Mandy had balked. "That's an awful story!"

"Shush! Let me finish. So, they were split up, yes? But that didn't mean he stopped loving her. Mistresses weren't an uncommon thing back then, especially in arranged marriages."

"And she was fine with playing second banana? Is that the moral of the story? I don't want to be anyone's tramp."

"No. The moral is she took what she could get within the constraints handed to her because she loved him that much. Was it ideal? No. But look how much came to bear from that union. You're here, right?"

"Whatever, Abi."

"You don't believe me?"

"I just assumed you made that royal lineage story up when I was a kid just to make me feel special."

"Oh, *mi abejorro*. What ever happened to you to have so little idea of your self-worth? Of course you're special, and not just because of lineage."

"I thought I *did* have a pretty good idea. It's been a rough few months. Still, I'm not playing secret lover with Aaron Owen anymore."

"Owen? Any relation to that woman Elly?"

Mandy had rubbed her eyes and sighed.

"Miranda, I know I taught you to pick your battles, but you're not picking the right ones. You love him?"

Mandy was silent, but Abi plowed on. "You need to figure out if what he's asking of you is all that unreasonable. If it is—fine. You'll move on. If not, figure out a way to make it work. *Besos.* I have a date with some cake."

The conversation had left Mandy feeling even more confused than when she'd started.

Michael stood with some difficulty. "Ugh. Well, speaking of cars, I need to get to work. I've got to go to an auction in Greenville today. Hope I don't run into Dad. That'd be awkward." He stretched his arms over his head and groaned when his back popped. "You working at the office today? We can carpool and I'll have Frank bring me home."

She picked the remote up, turned the channel to a morning news talk show and curled her legs up under her. "No. I'll probably work from home. I need to figure out how some of the part-time techs ended up with overtime last week."

"I don't envy you." Mike shuffled into the kitchen, deposited his mug into the sink, and limped toward the bathroom to shower.

"Right. Fun."

The truth was she had already figured out the overtime glitch. She was actually avoiding Aaron. They'd been communicating only in terse instant messages for most of the week. He had tried to call her once, but she quickly hit the ignore button on her phone and shut it off for the rest of the day.

Attempting to avoid him that day turned out to be a moot exercise when at eleven o'clock she realized she was missing about half the files she needed to update the employee handbook. She'd transferred them from Aaron's computer at work onto a thumb drive the week before and left them in her rarely occupied office. Or at least she *hoped.* She thought with it being nearly lunch he'd be out of the office, or perhaps on the road where he preferred to be.

That hope was dashed the moment she realized the thumb drive wasn't in *her* office at all, but his. She'd left it in there when she'd had to place some sticky note reminders on his computer monitor.

She backed into his office and closed the door as soundlessly as she could only to have a pair of large hands grip her around the waist and pull her against a warm, sandalwood-scented chest.

"I'm going to guess by the way you just leapt a mile into the air you weren't expecting me to be here." The rough pad of one of Aaron's fingers dipped into the collar of her shirt and edged down her shoulder. He grazed his lips down her neck and stopped at the place her bra strap should have been. "You're not wearing a bra?" He answered his own question by looking down the front of her casual tee-shirt dress.

She pushed her collar back up and edged away from his hold. "It's usually just the girls here during the day. I figured I'd just drop in and run right back out with what I needed."

When she finally turned around to get a look at him, she sucked in a breath. He was wearing a dark gray suit that seemed to have been cut precisely to his athletic build. Beneath the jacket was a crisp white shirt with the top three buttons undone. A light blue silk tie with a gray fleur de lis pattern hung around his neck. He looked damn good in Tar Heel blue for someone with such an aversion to the color.

He walked to his desk and leaned against the front edge, crossing his legs at the ankles. "And what do you need?"

"I've lost a thumb drive . . . that I need for . . . going somewhere?" she squeaked.

He made a beckoning gesture with his hands and she found herself walking forward without having given her feet the permission to do so. When they were toe-to-toe, he reached out to her and swept her long bangs out of her eyes.

"That's better. That's where you should be." He let his thumb linger, tracing a trail down the side of her face to her jaw and chin. "I have an important meeting with some potential financial backers. Funding may be a bigger issue come next year."

"Why?"

He smoothed his palm down to where the heart-shaped pendant on her necklace hung. He fingered it idly and let it fall back onto her chest. "My father thinks he can control me by controlling my grant eligibility."

"Do you need to be controlled?"

His palms crushed her breasts, pushing them up and together beneath the stretchy fabric of her dress. "No. I don't."

She could see a bulge forming at the front of his pants and impulsively put her hand over it.

"I missed you," he whispered, bringing his head down to the level of hers and locking his lips onto her mouth. He palmed her rear, scrunching the fabric of her dress up in his hands so her ass was exposed to the air. "When are you coming home?"

Home.

She whispered back, "We've already had this discussion."

"Give me an answer I want to hear, then." He nudged her panties down and parted her cheeks with his fingers. He silenced her with his kiss once more and moved one hand around to her front, tapping into the wetness of her sex and rubbing it onto her swollen nub. When his fingers breeched her tight entrance the only think keeping her from moaning loudly was his mouth over hers.

She placed trembling hands at the waist of his pants, fumbling with the belt and trying to work his button free. Somehow she managed to release the fastening without ripping it off and looked up into his eyes as she encircled her hands around his cock. The head was slick, and she shuddered at the accumulated memories of how many times it'd breached her before.

He seemed to be reading her thoughts, or perhaps something in her gaze impelled him, because he picked her up and set her back flat against the desktop. Seeming to change his mind, he backed off her just enough to slip his fingers under her sides, and turned her over, sliding her back to the edge so her ass was presented to him like a gift.

He slid into her in one easy thrust, the force of which made her try to dig her nails into the wooden desk. She thought she should feel brazen there over his desk with him pounding into her, but with him filling her the way she'd so desired for the past few sleepless nights she found it difficult to care about propriety.

"God, Miranda . . . please . . . "

"Please . . . what . . . Aaron?"

She was so close. So close to that brass ring—the queen of all orgasms. She could feel it forming in her loins and spreading upward to her breasts and all the way down to her clenched toes. Her breath had gone shallow, vision blurred, and she spilled over the edge when she felt his teeth clamping into the tender skin between her neck and shoulder. He jammed the heel of his hand against her mouth just in time to stifle her scream.

"What an awful knack of timing I have! I'll give you two a moment to tidy up," a deep, cheerful voice said from behind them just before the office door clicked closed.

CHAPTER 16

"I don't really have time to have this conversation right now," Aaron said as he knotted his tie by feel and glowered over his desktop at Rick. He had a lot of nerve coming into his place of business unannounced and into his office without even so much as a knock.

"I would imagine you don't have a lot of time for . . . " Rick fixed his stare on Mandy who was standing behind Aaron's chair at the moment and waved a hand in a dismissive fashion. "*Diversions* when you're at the office."

"It's none of your business, Rick." Aaron straightened his cufflinks and stood, pinching up the suit jacket draped on the back of his chair. Mandy stepped forward and grabbed the shoulders, holding it up so he could easily slip his arms into it. The gesture had seemed so automatic on her part, probably a leftover compulsion from working in a clothing store, but he appreciated the sweet gesture all the same. He offered her a small smile and was pretty sure there was a reddening of her cheeks before she turned her back to them. He turned his attention back to his father's dear old friend, his smile already gone.

"Oh, but it is my business, you see. That's my job, remember?" Rick pressed his palms onto the desk and leaned in close. "The public wants to know if your hands are clean, Aaron. Doesn't matter if Charles is attached to this outfit or not. People assume he is, so they're watching you. But you already knew that. Been good until now." He drummed the desktop with his fingers and pushed himself upright before pacing in front of the guest chairs. "You have to be above reproach. Squeaky clean. So, if you're screwing your staff, people are going to assume your sense of morality is a bit loose. Funny how the public is, huh?"

Aaron stared down at his hands for a moment, let his eyes blur on a spot where motor oil stained his cuticle, and took a deep breath. He wouldn't get loud. Not with so many staff members in earshot. He chose his words carefully.

"I hired Miranda after we became personally involved, not before."

Rick's shoulders bounced upward into an elegant shrug. "I'm not certain that makes it any better. Nepotism and such."

"It's not nepotism if she's the most qualified person for the job. And as you might have noticed, we've been quite discreet. Otherwise we would have had this confrontation before now, right?"

"I think your father is going to want to know about it." Rick spun on his expensive Italian heel and walked toward the door.

Shit.

He'd obviously driven all the way out to Durham for a reason, and whatever it was still wasn't apparent. Aaron hated to call him back, but . . .

"Rick, what did you want, anyway? I know you didn't come all the way out to Durham to play hall monitor."

Rick stopped, turned his gaze to Mandy briefly, then to Aaron. Aaron didn't like the way he'd looked at her—like some game that needed hunting. When Rick spoke again his voice was, low. Sibilant, even.

"Nothing. It's irrelevant now." He made another flicking gesture with his hand and left.

Mandy slipped in front of Aaron's desk chair and leaned her backside against the edge. He automatically wrapped his arms around her thighs.

"What does this mean?" she asked.

He rubbed her through the back of her skirt for a moment, then leaned back in his chair and slipped his pen out of his pants pocket. After threading it through his fingers for a while, he admitted, "I don't know, sweetheart. And at this point, I also don't care. Fuck it." He pushed his seat back and stood.

She narrowed her eyes and crossed her arms over his breasts. "You don't care about what exactly?"

He bobbed his head in the direction of the closed door. "That." He gave Mandy a gentle peck on the cheek and tucked her hair behind her ears. "Answer your phone when I call you, please."

Her expression was wary but she nodded. "Yeah."

Aaron left Mandy to the office where she appeared to be resuming her search for her thumb drive and he walked out to the reception area, thinking he owned Jasmine a stern talking to. For some reason, she always turned into a pile of goo every time that man walked into the office. What had he done to her? She was sweet, but usually don't let people bowl her over.

He found the reception area empty. The out-of-office greeting light was activated on her phone, so he figured she must have stepped out for lunch.

Rick stood from the wingback chair he'd sat and crossed his legs in and gestured to the door. "Decided to stick around. Shall we talk over lunch?"

Aaron ground his teeth and leaned over Jasmine's desk to pull a sticky note out of the dispenser. He clicked his pen and scribbled a note: *See Mandy later about establishing protocol for reception back up.*

When he stood again, his impulse was to say "no" straight out, but hearing Mandy rustling in his drawers several doors down gave him pause. If he was going to have it out with the man, they might as well do it in semi-private. That's what his mother would have had him do, anyway. She'd told him to be the captain of his own ship—the master of his own destiny. That if he didn't want the press to control him, then he'd better start controlling *them.*

He gave a curt nod. "Fine."

Aaron trailed Rick in his own car to a restaurant allowed the hostess to lead him and Rick to a back booth. Rick immediately put in an order for whiskey on the rocks. Given the early hour, Aaron abstained.

When Rick didn't seem to be forthcoming with the expected haranguing, Aaron tapped his fingers against the tabletop and said, "Well?"

Rick cleared his throat. "As you've already been counseled, next year's race is expected to be one of the tightest ever, even without us knowing who's going to be on the ticket. People are ready for change. Bad news for us."

"Yeah, I keep hearing that." Aaron swirled the ice in his water around so it made a complete circuit in the glass.

"Shy of having everyone hold their breath, we need everyone to be on their best behavior."

Aaron set down his glass and cracked his knuckles. "Say something new."

"Fine, how's this? I did some checking on your staff coordinator. Motley little family she has. Father was thrown out of the Army on his ear for insubordination about thirty years ago and now lives off the grid in the southwest. We're looking into that. Her mother's road to citizenship is a bit unusual in my opinion, if it's even legal. I have my doubts. Her stepfather—"

"I don't give a shit about her stepfather. Why are you doing background checks on my girlfriend, anyway?"

Rick scoffed and took a long sip of his drink. "Until this morning, we weren't aware of the exact nature of your relationship, not that it matters. We did a bit of checking on her because I was thinking about offering her a position with the campaign."

Aaron balled his napkin up into his fist and tried his hardest to squelch the urge to rip it to shreds. "You can't headhunt my people."

"Why not? Isn't that what you do? Swoop in to little ma and pa shops and steal their people? You did good. Looks and a brain. She's a political wet dream."

Aaron reached across the table, grabbed Rick's tie and yanked. "Don't you dare talk about Miranda like she's some kind of object. You want me to behave? You damn sure better act like it. Pass that on to Dad if you want. I'm not playing puppet anymore." He released the tie and stood. "And I pretty sure Miranda voted for the other guy three years ago."

Rick made a choking sound while he loosened the noose. "I guess you're not concerned about your funding for next year, are you Aaron?"

"You let me worry about the funding. You just worry about that contract you obviously signed with Mephistopheles, 'cause you'll have to pay up your end eventually. Enjoy your bloody steak, you fucking vampire."

*

"Tell me about these people and why I should hire them."

Mandy sat in the conference room of CTW with the headquarters staff feeling slightly ill at ease at the seating arrangement. Aaron had pointedly followed her into the room on her heels and took the seat immediately adjacent to her. He'd even gone as far as to share her handouts. His behavior was an odd reversal to her.

Mike spoke up first. He really was good at being the volunteer. "Luciano Gurka. My old roommate from UNC-W. He currently lives down in Florence. He flipped houses until he became a millionaire then the market softened. He's been living on savings for the past couple of years, but he's ready to go back to work."

"He's motivated? He'd be in that zone all by himself."

"Hell yeah. He's got a new wife and a little baby. He's the kind of guy if you give him a short string he'll find a way to turn it into a sweater."

"Great. Miranda, can you get him up here for an interview? You'll need to jibe it with my schedule as well as yours."

"Got it."

"Anyone else?"

Mandy put up her hand, felt silly for doing it, then put it down. "My friend Chelsea expressed an interest several weeks ago. I thought perhaps she was pulling my leg, but she got in touch with me again last week wanting to know how to formally apply. She sent her résumé and some references over."

Aaron gave her a warm smile that made her cheeks burn. She didn't feel like she deserved it, especially not with the conversation she intended to have with him.

"What is she aiming to do? Screen?"

"Yes. She doesn't have experience working with NPOs, but she has spent the past four years doing social work. She's at the burnout point now."

"I'm surprised she lasted *that* long," Tina said from the opposite end of the table. "I only lasted two."

"Well, if her background's anything like Tina's, bring her in. Is she willing to travel?"

Mike chuckled. "Oh yeah, I'll answer that. I believe her exact phrase was 'I'm single and ready to mingle.' She has no attachments whatsoever and could spend days on the road if she had to."

"Good. She'd need to meet with me and Tina. Schedule it?"

Mandy nodded.

"Anyone else?"

Several other people put names of friends and loved ones they thought deserved a chance forward. Aaron approved them all for an interview except one who hadn't quite been released from jail yet. Once they'd run out of people to refer, he asked her to put up some ads.

"That's it, folks. See you at next month's meeting unless you need me before then. Miranda, thank you, sweetheart."

Jasmine raised a brow for a fleeting moment, but busied herself with clearing away trash from the conference room.

Michael was the last to stand.

"Hey, Mirandy, you wanna go get some lunch? Don said he would be driving through on his way back from Asheville."

Aaron piped up before she could answer. "Sorry, Mike. I'm taking her to lunch."

She dropped the stack of papers she was holding and felt her stomach flop. "You are?" she asked from her crouched position. *What's he doing?*

"I think I owe my girl a hot meal. She's shriveling up."

She looked down at what she could see of her body. "I am?"

Mike was silent.

"You work too hard, sweetheart. Hey, Mike—why don't you offer to buy Eleanor and Tina lunch? They're always looking for someone to mooch off, and I think they consider you sucker enough."

Mike shifted his weight to his good leg and managed a dry chuckle. "Do I get anything in return for my generosity?"

"Yes, they might let you control the radio station the next time you're in the van together."

Mike made a little *whoopee do* gesture with his hand, but smiled and picked up his cane. "I'll see you at home, Mirandy."

"Yeah, I'll see you after din—"

Aaron gave her ass a silencing pinch. "Sorry. She's going home with me. Looks like you'll have the apartment all to yourself."

Mike furrowed his forehead.

She looked from her stepbrother to Aaron, who was giving the ginger a cool look. "Um . . . "

"Wanna meet me in the SUV, Mandy? I'll be out in a minute," Aaron said with a cheerful voice.

She opened her mouth, closed it without saying anything, clutched her papers to her chest, and hurried out. The tension was so thick in the room that whatever was about to go down, she didn't want to be within twenty feet of the fallout. They were big boys. They could take care of themselves whatever the problem was. She hoped. She hoped it wasn't a car problem. She couldn't help with that.

*

Mike leaned against the closed office door and crossed his arms over his chest. "Are you seriously fucking around with Mandy?"

Aaron put his feet up on his desk and crossed his legs at the ankles. "Whether or not we're fucking is none of your business. Am I pulling her chain? From this moment forward, no. No, I'm not."

"What exactly is that supposed to mean?"

"It means I'm not going to let anyone tell me how to live my life and who should be in it. I love Mandy and I intend to marry that woman. Do you have a problem with that, Mike?"

Mike's bottom jaw ground left to right.

Aaron's curled his lips into a smirk. "You carrying a bit of a torch for her?"

Mike scoffed, hobbled to the armchairs in front of Aaron's desk and sank into one. "Let's put it this way. I've known her since before our parents hooked up. I've had an awareness that she was a pretty girl and that I was a hot-blooded boy since middle school. Of course I had a crush on her. Everyone did. She's just one of those people that others notice. But then Dad met Adriana and there was this hush-hush super-quick courtship, and *boom*. They were married."

He cracked his knuckles and looked at Aaron over them. "She's my best friend. She's smart and funny and kind. She's a truly decent person, and I couldn't love her more even if were blood siblings. That's why I've been steering boys away from her since I was in tenth grade."

Aaron twirled his pen in his fingers then tossed it at Mike who caught it handily. "I've been carrying that pen around for about three years. It was from the first batch of bills my father signed into law after inauguration."

"It's a nice pen." Mike stuck it into his own pocket with a smirk.

"Yeah. All these years I've been carrying it around as a reminder of who I'm supposed to be. How I should act."

"You giving up?"

"On Miranda? No way. I don't want to be some forty-year-old man who regrets the things he didn't do ten years before because he was waiting for permission from someone who was never going to give it. Miranda may not be cut from the kind of cloth Rick and my father like, but I think it drapes me pretty well."

Mike tented his fingers and nodded. "If you hurt her, I'll fuck you up."

"Is that what you told all the other guys? The ones that dumped her?"

"Yes."

"And I take it you've made good on that threat before or else they wouldn't believe it."

Mike held out his hands and shrugged.

Aaron grinned. "Good to know. Really. Go buy Eleanor lunch. I think she likes you."

Mike smirked. "Wow, you're actually not afraid of me. You must be like King Arthur pulling that sword out of the stone. You pass the test."

"I'm worried less about the gatekeeper than what it's keeping me from."

And it was true. Mike's consent in the scheme of things meant nothing if Mandy wouldn't have him.

"Go on," he nudged. "I happen to know Eleanor has a Mike Leonard mini-poster taped inside her toolbox. She wouldn't say no if you offered to buy her a meal."

Mike stood with some effort. "Well, maybe I can show her some of my tricks."

Aaron laughed and walked him to the door. "Godspeed."

CHAPTER 17

Mandy was standing next to the front passenger door of the SUV, digging through her purse for her lipstick when a long black car pulled up next to her in the CTW lot. The driver, an older man with gray hair wearing dark sunglasses, rolled down his window. "Miss McCarthy?"

She squinted at the man. "I'm sorry, can I help you?"

He opened the door and stepped out. He reached for her elbow. She drew back.

"Miss McCarthy, if you'd join the governor in the vehicle, you'd do him a great boon."

She took another step backward. "The governor? I'm sorry, if you want to speak with Aaron," she hooked her thumb in the direction of CTW's back door, "he's inside the building. He'll be out here shortly."

One of the rear passenger windows motored down. Rick's face appeared in the opening. "We don't want to talk to Aaron. We want to talk to *you*."

"You can set an appointment with Jasmine in the office. I'm very busy."

A second head appeared in the window, this time one that made her feel like her heart stopped beating.

"Yes, I'm sure you are, Miss McCarthy, but certainly you understand that I am as well?"

She looked to the back door and saw no one darkening the hall. Where was Aaron? What had held him up? She wrapped her fingers around her phone inside her purse and toggled up the speed dial screen to Aaron's number. She let it ring without putting it to her ear.

"I don't think I need to get inside that car to have a conversation with you, sir."

"No, no. Of course not, but certainly you understand how valuable privacy is?"

She cut her gaze to Rick. "That's rich coming from you."

"I'm truly sorry for causing you any embarrassment, Miss McCarthy. It wasn't my intention to intrude on anything so . . . " Rick waved a hand around while he fumbled for the words. "Personal."

"Do you regularly make a habit of barging in on other businesses that have nothing to do with you and manhandling the staff?"

"Well, manhandling's a strong word. We'd just like to *discuss* some things with you."

"You're not going to discuss anything with her."

Finally, Aaron to the rescue. He used the remote clicker to unlock the doors of the SUV and helped Mandy up into her seat. He offered his father, Rick, and the driver a rude gesture just before shutting her door.

The limo was still idling there when Aaron climbed up into the driver's seat and started the ignition. He turned to her and gave her a winning smile. "So, lunch? I know a great little vegetarian place downtown. Best flatbread you'll ever sink your teeth into."

"Are you taking me out on a date?"

"Yes, I am. Later, we can move your things back into my apartment. My toothbrush has been really lonely in its little cup without yours."

"Uh, hold up a minute here." Mandy watched the limo following them in the side mirror. "What is this sudden change of heart?"

"My heart's always been the same. It's my degree of courage that's changed. Do you like falafel?"

"I'd prefer chicken nuggets."

Aaron blanched. "Ugh."

"You don't eat meat?" She had to think back on it. All those nights at his apartment he'd let her order what she wanted, and when pizza came he always picked his pepperoni off without complaint. Why hadn't he just asked her to order cheese?

"No, except under duress. I haven't eaten a chicken nugget or a hot dog since seventh grade. I'll tell you that story one day when it's not lunchtime."

"How do you get that big not eating meat?"

He wiggled his brows.

"Ugh! Not what I meant." She slumped in her seat and covered her face with her hands as the limo pulled up in the lane beside them. She peeked through her fingers at the driver. "Aaron?"

"Yeah, I see 'em."

"Is this about to turn into a Lady Di and Dodi Fayed situation?"

"Nah." He swung a hard U-turn, cut across a couple of lanes of traffic, and steered the SUV onto I-40 West. "Let's see 'em keep up with that. Pretty sure I get better gas mileage."

"What difference does your gas mileage make?"

He cocked a brow up at her over the top of his mirrored sunglasses. He didn't explain, but two and a half hours later they were burning rubber into Chowan County and the limo finally stopped for gas.

"Heh heh."

"Aaron, of all the places you could have driven, why here? You could have driven in circles around Durham."

He shrugged and motored on toward the rural county. "I guess I was feeling nostalgic."

She studied the countryside around whipping past through her window. "Are we—?"

"Yes. I actually have a blanket this time. Figured you'd like to make love horizontally."

She felt a hot blaze behind her cheeks and crossed her legs in the other direction. She checked the mirror on her side. No one behind them.

He pulled into that secret driveway.

She waited there in her seat until he got out on his side, fetched something from the cargo area, and walked around to her door to assist her.

"What's that expression on your face all about?" he asked, smirking as he unfastened her seatbelt.

"If I didn't know any better, I'd think you planned this."

"No, sweetheart. I just know an opportunity when I see one. I am the offspring of a politician, after all."

His phone rang and he pulled it out of his pant's pocket, glanced at the display, and then shoved it into the glove compartment without answering. He held his elbow out to her. "Come on, sweetheart. Old time's sake? You'll never know when we'll ever have a chance to come back out this way."

Now her phone rang. She held up a finger to still him and regarded the number flashing on the screen. "It's my mother. She never calls me."

"Think it's important?"

She muted the phone and shrugged. "If it is, she'll leave a message. Maybe Archie's bad karma finally caught up to him and he needs bail money or a blood donation or something." She stuffed her phone into the glove compartment to join Aaron's.

"Miranda, you're the most compassionate woman I've ever met. Your generosity makes me want to strive to be a better man. Marry me." His face was very serious. She stared at him for a full minute then both burst into laughter.

He spread a large beach blanket on the overgrown grass and used his feet to mash down the ridges. He smiled at her as he unbuttoned his shirt and heeled off his brogues. "You know, sweetheart, there's a vegetarian festival in Moore Square this weekend. We should go."

She took a step forward and relieved him of his belt. "That sounds interesting." Actually, it didn't sound interesting at all. She loved meat. Especially meat that had once oinked. She did, however, like the idea of flitting around town on the arm of arguably the sexiest man in the state. Hell, *country.*

"Or if it's more your thing, there's a muscadine celebration Mom was going to drag me to by my ear. She's got to make a speech. We could all go together."

She raised one brow at him as he peeled her light sweater over her head. "Your mother?"

"Yeah. She knows." He drew her in close and pressed hot lips against the crook of her neck. "And Elly."

Mandy tipped her head back to let him access the erogenous area over her throat. He handily released the clasp of her bra and flicked the offensive undergarment away. "And your father, obviously."

"Yeah, he's not so important."

"I'm sure millions of people would disagree."

He pushed her skirt down to her ankles along with her panties before giving her ass an appreciative caress. "I'm only worried about the person in front of me right now." He kicked his pants along with his briefs to the side and pulled her down to the ground with him. He laced his fingers through her hair and pulled her close, searching her mouth her tongue as he leaned back against the blanket.

She edged backward down his torso until his erection nudged her swollen clit. He lifted her up and eased her slowly down onto his shaft.

"I love how you're always ready."

"Hard not to be given the cause of my arousal," she said, bracing her knees at his sides and planting her hands on his chest for leverage.

"God, you're perfect." He skimmed his hands up her sides

from her waist to her breasts, pausing there to apply the pads of this thumbs to her perked nipples.

She let a grin span her face as she bent down to reach his lips. "Save it for when I'm dressed."

"I'll tell you again and again, Miranda." He tucked her bottom lip between his teeth and drew it out, scraping it gently as she pulled back. He tightened his grip on her ass, forcing more of himself into her sex, increasing the pace of their joining.

She closed her eyes and let herself go at the same time he rolled her to her side and pulled out to aim the product of their coupling into the grass.

"I appreciate that," she said, panting as she stared up into the Carolina blue sky.

He lay back with her, scooping her in close to his side and studying the few fluffy white clouds along with her. "Long ride back to Durham. Wanted you to be comfortable."

*

As Mandy dexterously fastened the buttons of Aaron's shirt there in the open door of the SUV, he checked his voicemails. He listened once, groaned, and replayed the message on speaker. He held it out for her.

"Aaron, this is your father. Rick and I are at A-1 Autos. We'll be waiting here for you as long as necessary. If I were you I wouldn't try passing us by." He tucked his shirt in and fastened his belt while Mandy retrieved her own phone from the glove box.

He watched her blanch, and then blush as she listened to her own messages. She requeued it and held it out to him. It was her mother.

"Mandy, the governor is here. We need to talk. I don't understand why you're doing this. There are other men."

Her hands shook as she ended the call and tucked her phone

away. Her face was set with shock, even a sort of revulsion he didn't understand.

"So, what do we do?" Mandy scraped her bangs back from her eyes and held them in place with her sunglasses.

Aaron helped her up into the passenger seat and laid a kiss on her lips before shutting her door. "I'm not going to be bullied." He growled as he walked around the front of the SUV, getting the vitriol out of his system so that by the time he climbed into the driver's seat, he was all smiles and charm.

They rode to AA1A in silence. When he noticed her wringing her hands, he wrapped his right hand around hers and squeezed. "Sweetheart, everything will be fine."

"Aaron, if this is going to—"

"Shh." He parked right in front of the trailer steps and killed the engine. "Stop it."

*

Adriana watched them from the door of the hospitality lounge, a scowl marring her pretty face.

"Shall we?" he asked, hitting the door lock switch.

Mandy sighed then shrugged. "Might as well get it over with."

They walked hand-in-hand up the concrete block steps and through the door Mom held open.

Archie was sitting at the end of one of the Naugahyde sofas with his arms folded over his distended belly. "I knew that little bitch would get me in trouble eventually. No better than her father."

Aaron took a step forward seemingly impulsively, but Mandy yanked him back.

"Don't."

"Now, now, Mr. Leonard," Rick said from his perch on the adjacent sofa. "As we've said, Miss McCarthy is quite lovely. It's just this is a delicate situation for the governor."

"I'm having a hard time understanding how my and Mandy's relationship merits this conference."

The governor stood and pushed his shirtsleeves up his forearms as he strolled over to his son. "Aaron, understand I always know more than you."

"Meaning what?"

"I'm not saying Miss McCarthy has been withholding information from you, but there are things you don't know that can mar my reputation. She probably doesn't know herself."

"This is getting tedious," Mandy said, shrugging out from Aaron's hold. "All parties in attendance—spit it out."

"I like a woman who shoots straight from the hip," Rick said.

"Yeah, me too," Aaron said, letting his brows knit.

"Fine, fine. Let's lay it all out here so Mr. Leonard can get back to the business of managing his car lot." The governor walked over to Mandy and put a hand on her shoulder. She didn't draw back. Of all the things she had to be afraid of, he wasn't one of them.

"Mandy, my dear, are you aware your father—your *biological* father, I mean—has several wives?"

She looked from Charles to her mother, eyes narrowed. Mom shrugged. "We were never legally married. I didn't know it at the time. He always kept us separate. When I didn't agree to join the bunch, he left."

There was her confirmation. She suspected as much after listening to that voicemail. If her mother thought one man was interchangeable for the next, she had never been in love. The realization had hit Mandy like a ton of bricks, but now she was just pissed. Mom didn't even care that he'd left. He was just a means to an end.

"Well, there you go," Mandy said, voice low and flat. "I haven't seen my father since I was seven. We don't communicate."

"Ah," the governor reached out a hand to give her a pat, but she backed up a step.

"Well, Mandy, he doesn't try so hard to hide it nowadays. Gets around that sticky legal issue by being married on paper to one of the women. The rest live in his household quite comfortably. I'm sure you can see how this would muddle people's understanding of the values espoused by my campaign."

She shook her head. "No, actually I can't. It's a tenuous association at best. A man I don't speak to engages in a practice you find distasteful? So what?"

"Ah, but you see—it's easy for information like that to become twisted once it becomes public knowledge. The next thing you know, people will think Aaron appreciates that lifestyle, and by extension," he put up his shoulders in a shrug, "me."

Aaron cracked his knuckles and shoved his fists into the pockets of his slacks. "So, what am I supposed to do? Not love her?" He turned to Mom. "Adriana, don't you want Mandy to be happy?"

"I don't want her involved in a scandal, do you? That wouldn't be good for any of us. What's the point of letting all those skeletons out of the closet? Let them lie."

Aaron shook his head and made a brisk walk across the room to take Mandy's hand. "Listen to yourselves. Maybe Elly had it right all along."

Rick scoffed and stretched his arms over his head, yawning. "Right. The girl with the IQ of a ladybug, now procreating. We should all follow her lead."

Aaron took another involuntary step forward. Mandy shoved her hand into the waistband of his slacks and gave him a yank. It was enough.

"Dad, too far."

Charles put up his hands. "You're right. Rick, please."

Rick shrugged.

Mom put her hands on Mandy's shoulder and gave her a pleading look. "Miranda, please. The governor has done a lot of good for the people of North Carolina. Just think about it, will you? Can you put your desires aside for a little while? Until after the election?"

Aaron pulled Mandy back to him and held her against his chest, but for some reason she didn't feel comforted.

"No. The election is next fall. Then what? You tell us to toe the line another three years while Dad gets his shit together for national office? I don't think so. Come on, Miranda."

"If you go without resolving this to my satisfaction," Charles said, sinking into the seat beside Rick on the sofa, "there's your funding."

"You're not welcome back here, Mandy, so you better make sure he takes care of you," Archie barked.

Aaron's hand squeezed tighter around hers as he pulled her toward the door.

Mom trailed them out and watched as Aaron helped Mandy into his SUV. She grabbed the door handle before he could push the door closed.

"Mandy, please. Think about what this is going to do to Archie."

Mandy laughed, sounding somewhat hysterical and not caring. "Archie? Who gives a shit about Archie? Not me. Not anymore. What kind of deals has he been cutting with the governor in the past hour, huh? Gonna funnel some money his way somehow? Overlook his tax filings? Get him some permits?"

Mom shook her head and clucked her tongue. "Mandy, Archie took care of us when there was no one. The least you could do is help out."

"What are you talking about? There was always Abi."

Mom mumbled something low and gutteral in Spanish, the gist of which was about Abi stifling her freedom, which Mandy found ironic given her situation.

"She wouldn't understand. Because of Archie, we didn't have to move back to Spain after your father left. He made it so we could stay here."

"You're full of sh—"

Aaron closed the door on Mandy's commentary.

Adriana, blank-faced on the other side of the glass, had nothing further to say.

CHAPTER 18

"What's wrong, sweetheart?"

Mandy had been pensive since returning to Durham, her mind constantly churning with what had happened back in Edenton. She'd called her grandmother for counsel, and all Abi could offer for reassurance was, "I'll kill them." That had made Mandy laugh, but it hadn't lifted her spirits for long. She felt like some sort of outcast of her own making—one who could potentially ruin the life of the man she thought she loved. What does one do in that sort of bind?

She plucked a French fry from the basket they shared at Elmo's Diner and shook her head. "Nothing. Just thinking about those interviews from this morning."

Aaron watched her for a moment wordlessly then took a bite of his bean cake sandwich. "Screenings didn't go well?" He'd been out of the office for the past couple of days and had just gotten back into town. He'd been talking with potential major donors, looking for funding sources to make up for the deficit he expected Cars to Work to face in the coming year.

"They were okay. I'm just worried their personalities won't jibe with the rest of the crew."

He shrugged. "It's an important concern, for sure, but as the charity gets bigger, we may not have the luxury of ensuring everyone on each team is simpatico."

"That's true." She swirled the French fry again without even having taken a bite from the first time she dipped it.

"Miranda?"

"Hmm?"

"Is there anything else upsetting you?" He put his sandwich

down and reached across the tabletop to grab her hands.

She drew back. "Aaron, I . . . " She took a deep breath and let the words come out in one mumbled stream. "I guess I'm putting in my notice. I can't do this."

He shook his head. "What are you talking about? I'm about to promote everyone including you."

"Aaron, I . . . I just don't feel I can keep up with you. We're on completely different levels?" She didn't mean for it to sound like a question, but she hadn't rehearsed the lie enough times for it to come out the way she wanted.

He stood. "Woman, what are you talking about?"

She slipped out of her side of the bench and walked briskly to the door. There was a bus coming. She intended to be on it. He tried to follow but the waitress caught up. "Sir, your bill?"

He stopped. "Miranda!"

She rushed outside the restaurant and onto the city bus when it stopped at the corner. As she dropped coins into the receptacle, she looked through the door's glass panels to see him standing by their table, his jaw slack as if he'd just been slapped.

*

Ten days later, Mandy was sitting in her apartment on the sofa, feet on the coffee table and her CTW laptop propped on her lap. It was the last time she'd have to enter payroll figures or schedule screening appointments. It'd be someone else's chore in a few days, she figured.

Other than to buy groceries and walk the quarter mile to her mailbox, she hadn't left the apartment. Mike had been trying to coax her out, insisting it was safe to work out of the office because Aaron wasn't there, but she didn't believe him.

She closed the laptop lid and flicked on the television. Mike had left it on some news station and there on the screen was the governor bloviating about fiscal something-or-other. She rolled her eyes and flipped through the channels, finally settling on a Mexican soap opera. She understood about every other word.

She had actually been giving some thought to moving to Spain after she tidied up her loose ends with CTW. It'd been Abi's idea. "What else you gonna do, huh? Sit around and sulk? You're young. Live your life. Come live with me. I'll make sure you have fun," Abi had said. "Don't worry about the money. You want money? I'll give you some. Why you don't ask?"

"Mom said to never ask."

Abi had mumbled something in Spanish Mandy hadn't quite caught, but the gist didn't cast Mom in a good light.

Keys jangled just outside the door and Mike and Eleanor fell into the apartment, laughing.

"Hey, Mandy!" Eleanor straightened up, tucking her mussed shirt into her jeans.

"Hey." Mandy looked at the clock on the cable box. Lunchtime. She stood up and padded to the refrigerator in her sheepy pajamas and fuzzy socks.

"What are you doing here?" Mike asked, closing the door. "Aren't you supposed to be meeting with that vendor about employee badges?"

She stuck her head into the fridge, scanning the shelves for the baggie full of bacon she'd put away. "Nope. Not my job."

"Uh, yeah it's your job. At least until Monday."

She shrugged. She gave up on finding the bacon after remembering she'd eaten it as a 3 A.M. snack the *second* time she'd woken up from dreaming about Aaron. The first time she'd pounded her head against the pillow until she'd fallen back asleep.

"Come on, Mandy, you can't be seriously quitting just like that." Eleanor climbed up onto one of the tall barstools at the kitchen counter and leaned her elbows onto the countertop.

Mandy pulled out a block of cheddar and closed the door. She nodded. "Yes, I can. It's too awkward."

"How?" Mike took the cheese, which Mandy was unsuccessfully trying to unwrap with her thumbnails, and found the easy-open tab. He peeled the plastic off and handed it back to her. "You work mostly from home. You'd see Aaron once per month for staff meetings or whenever you'd have to go in to conduct interviews."

Mandy cut her gaze toward Eleanor.

"She knows," Mike said. "It's not a secret. Everyone in the office knows."

"Yeah," Eleanor agreed. She pulled a cheese knife out of the block and handed it to Mandy. "And everyone in the office thinks you're an idiot."

Mandy chopped off a giant hunk of cheese, ate it, and followed it immediately with a bite of rustic bread she'd torn right off the loaf. "Okay, so maybe awkward's not the right word to use. Maybe devastating is a better word. Fuck, is that better for y'all?"

Mike drew her into a hug. "Aw, honey. I know what it's like to love someone you can't have."

"You do?"

"Sure, I do. I've been there. But that's not what you're dealing with. You can have him. This is a matter of choice. *Your* choice. He's been clear the ball's in your court, hasn't he?"

She shrugged. "Dunno. I don't listen to his voicemails."

He gave her a little shake. "Ugh. You're hopeless."

She took another bite of cheese and sidled away to grab a green apple out of the basket. "Exactly. I'm doing what's best for him." She shuffled toward her bedroom.

"Oh, I see," Mike called after her. "Well, don't forget you have a job fair you're supposed to represent CTW at tomorrow."

She froze. She *had* forgotten. "Shit."

"Yeah, that. Oh, package came for you." He tapped it on the counter. "Hey, Eleanor. You want a cheese sandwich?"

*

Mandy yawned and picked up the last of the boxes of pamphlets and swag. She nestled it into her tight car trunk and slammed the lid shut. She wiped her hands off on her black slacks and rooted in her hipster purse for her keys. The purse was new. The funky gray and black bag had been in the mail Mike had brought up the day before. She knew a bribe when she saw one, but she couldn't fault Mrs. Owen for her chutzpah. It wasn't like she was going to send it back. It was special edition.

"Damn it." She opened her purse wider but couldn't see the glint of metal inside. "Maybe I left them on the seat."

She opened the passenger door and found her keys there on the floorboard. "Ah."

Aaron slipped into the driver's side with some effort and pushed the seat back.

She startled. Where the Hell had he come from so quietly?

He shut the door and pulled the seatbelt across his chest, offering her that winning smile that she had found so charming the day they met at Archie's lot.

"How about we take a little test drive and check out the struts on this thing?"

"Aaron, I have somewhere to be. Can you move?"

"Oh, I know. Job fair. I shuffled my schedule a bit. I can go."

"Oh. Well, have fun." She shut the door.

He rolled down the window. "Get in the car, Miranda. We're going together."

She snorted. "The Hell we are. I quit, remember? We broke up? Or, whatever people who aren't really together do."

Anger flashed in his eyes. "We *were* together, and you know it. Get in the car."

She stood there with her arms crossed over her chest, unmoving.

He sighed, put the parking brake on, and got out. He walked

around to her, grabbed her by the arms without a word, and stared into her eyes for a few moments. Then he folded her into the passenger seat. "I wish you had back doors. I'd put the child safety lock on," he mumbled while pulling her seatbelt across her body.

She crossed her arms over her chest again and briefly considered jumping out while he made his way back to the driver's side, but figured it'd be pointless. It was *her* car after all. She'd be stuck either way.

He got in and set the car on the road. They rode in silence for a while, and then he rested a hand atop her left knee. She looked down at it, but didn't push it away. "I missed you, sweetheart."

"Oh?"

"Of course. I love you, Miranda. I really do."

Her face burned and pulse pounded in her ears.

Oh my God. Fuck. What now?

She shifted her lips to the right side of her face and chewed the inside of her mouth. She stopped suddenly, remembering she'd all but given up that habit in recent weeks. Her stress level had gone way down after leaving AA1A. After meeting *Aaron*. Hell, her life had improved in a lot of ways, and not just carnal ones.

They rode in silence a while longer, but when he missed the exit he was supposed to take, she tapped his hand. "Uh, Aaron."

"Shh. I know where I'm going."

"Do you? The next exit is three miles past the road we need to get on."

He didn't answer. He missed the next exit, and the one after it, too. When he did turn off, they were somewhere in the middle of Bumfuck and Podunk and behind schedule. He parked the car on a quiet street in a small, quaint Piedmont town and seemed to be looking around for something. He unbuckled his seatbelt.

"Aaron?"

"Don't worry. Never worry with me."

>33

*

Aaron looked around the lot for evidence of the silver sedan and found it parked in a primo space right in front of the office. Typical. "Ah. Come on, sweetheart. Get your purse."

"Why?"

"You need your I.D."

He reached under the driver's seat, pulled out a manila envelope, and grabbed Mandy by the arm.

She put the brakes on their egress and swatted him. "For what? Tell me now or I'm not moving from this spot."

He laughed. God, he loved that prickly little woman.

"You really think I couldn't just pick your little ass up and carry you?"

She tapped the toe of her pump against the concrete walkway. "Could and should do not equate."

"Mom's waiting on us." He crooked his thumb toward the squat municipal building. "She's inside."

She raised a brow and clutched her new purse protectively. "Your mother? Why?"

"Just trust me. *Please?*" He clamped the envelope under his arm and pressed his hands together as if to pray.

She narrowed her eyes but finally shrugged her shoulders.

He looped his free arm around her waist and escorted her up the walkway.

"I kind of feel like I'm being marched to the gallows."

Something like that.

Mom met them in the small lobby and he watched Mandy's gaze immediately land on his mother's purse. It was from the new line. He gave Mandy's arm a nudge with his elbow to wake her up.

"Hello, Miranda," Mom said, pressing Mandy into a hug. She blotted at her eyes with a crumbled up tissue.

"What's wrong?" Mandy cocked her head to the side and

furrowed her brow. "What happened? Did someone die?"

Mom's voice went high and keening. "No, I always cry at weddings."

"Do what now?"

He gave Mandy a nudge toward the counter. "Heh. Don't mind Mom, sweetheart."

He pressed a mostly completed form and a couple of supporting documents onto the counter and handed her a pen. "Sign right there." He turned his attention to the clerk. "Magistrate on the way?"

"Yep. She was trying to find her stamp."

"Aaron, how'd you get a copy of my birth certificate?"

He chuckled. "Mike got it for me. Remind me to thank your mother for storing yours with his."

"Mike?"

"Yeah, I'm here!" Mike hobbled in through the door leaning heavily on his cane, Eleanor in his wake.

"What are you doing here?"

"You needed one more witness." He winked then collapsed onto a hard orange plastic chair.

Mandy put her hands on her hips again. "Aaron?"

"Yes, sweetheart?"

"You have something you want to tell me?"

"Yes."

"What?"

"We're getting married."

She shook her head. "No. We're not."

He was nonplussed. "I know I didn't read you wrong, Miranda. You're not a big wedding kind of girl. You're the secret elopement type. I figured I'd do you a solid and just skip the asking step."

"Oh, you *figured*, huh?"

Mom stepped in between them, still dabbing her eyes. "Don't you love him?"

Mandy looked from Mom to Aaron. He tried to wipe the smirk off his face and failed. Who was he kidding?

"Do ya, sweetheart?"

"Yes," she answered, voice so small as to be almost inaudible.

He pulled the pen closer to the edge. "Sign it. This is me taking a stand, sweetheart. No one but me is going to decide what makes me happy, and you're it."

She picked up the pen, tentatively. "But . . . *married*? What about—"

He gave her a squeeze. "Honeymoon in Spain, perhaps?"

The tightness in her jaw softened, but she still wasn't signing. "What about your dad's campaign? And CTW's funding?"

"Oh, screw the campaign. I'm sick of hiding my light under a bushel. And I'll fund CTW myself if I have to," Mom said. She started digging around in her giant purse.

"Sweetheart, don't worry about that. I've got a bunch of pokers in the fire. The organization isn't going bust anytime soon. Even if it means we have to sell chilidogs to raise funds." He made a *blech* face.

Mandy laughed. "Well, then, if you put it like that! Where do I sign?"

CHAPTER 19

"Are you sure you really want to do this? I mean, this way?"

Mandy twirled her rings around her finger and chewed the inside of her mouth. Aaron appeared to be cool as a cucumber, which somehow made her even *more* apprehensive.

"Oh yeah." He slung an arm around her shoulder and gave her a squeeze. "Kill all the speculation at once then head out for Madrid with the press approximately 65 percent less interested in my love life."

"Your father is going to kill you."

"Not until after the election." He gave her a little pat on the rear and nudged her toward the entrance into the packed meeting room. Flashes lit the room as photographers caught their arrival.

Mandy slipped in behind the long white-cloth-covered table and sat to the immediate left of her stepbrother. She made an appreciative grunt at the title printed on the placard in front of him.

"Congratulations, I guess. Development director? Fancy!"

Mike wriggled his brows. "Thanks, I'm feeling pretty fancy."

"What's Archie think?"

"Ooh! Let me answer!" Tina, at Mike's right, tapped the tabletop in front of him for attention. "I heard the entire exchange through the phone speaker. Archie's loud, huh?"

Mandy cringed. "Understatement."

"I believe, and correct me if I misheard, Michael, his instruction was for Mike to blow it out his ass. Apparently he thinks Mike is bad for business."

Mandy nodded, considering. "Yep. That sounds like Archie."

Jasmine scampered up, panting, right at the one-minute-before-showtime mark and placed paper name tents in front of Aaron and Mandy respectively. "Sorry about that! I truncated the letters in Mandy's name. That would have looked bad, people thinking I can't spell." She darted away. Mandy turned the placard around.

"Hey! I have a new title, too."

Aaron sat back and crossed his arms over his chest, smirking. "Two new titles. I think the unwritten one is more important, though."

"Yeah, *you* would."

The reporters on the front row went quiet, studying the signs. Hands started going up.

Aaron ignored them and got down to business. "I thank everyone for their continued interest in Cars to Work and the growth our organization is currently experiencing. Today I'm going to speak briefly about some of our recent corporate partnerships and what our expansion plans are. First I'd like to introduce some of my key staff members. At the end is Tina Hoye, who's been with me since the start of CTW. She is our training director and will be overseeing the competency of all the staff we're hiring. Beside her is Michael Leonard, our development director. He's come on board to help us plan our future programs. You can ask him any questions you'd like about how we go about procuring and distributing cars. You all know Miranda. She's our COO. Just call her 'chief.' She likes that."

Laughter filled the room.

"Now, I'd hate to rush this thing but I've got nonrefundable plane tickets for tonight and I haven't packed my suitcase yet."

The reporters in the room waited patiently while Aaron ran down his talking points for about fifteen minutes. When he was done, he took a deep breath and leaned back in his chair. "Any questions?"

Every person in the room put up a hand.

"Well, let's just start first row and go left to right." He pointed to the woman closest to the door. "Yep?"

"I'm sorry, just for the sake of accuracy, your COO's surname—"

"Is correct." He pointed to the next person. "Yeah?"

"Uh, and by *correct* you mean correct as printed on the name card?"

"Yes. Miranda Owen." He pointed to the next person.

"Um . . . " The man looked down at his notebook and seemed to have forgotten whatever it was he was going to ask.

"Next?"

"Yes, I'm from the *Indy*."

"Oh, boy," Tina mumbled.

"First of all, congratulations?"

"Thank you," Aaron and Mandy said in unison.

The woman made a note. "Second, as you're married to your COO, how are you going to handle oversight issues?"

"The same way I handled them when I was CEO, COO, CFO, phone grunt, mechanic, coffee guy, and delivery boy all in one. And while we're on the subject of transparency, I'd like to make it obvious that Mr. Leonard is my brother-in-law."

Hands went down. More popped up.

Aaron pointed to the next person. "Yes?"

The man cleared his throat. "Mr. Owen, how much involvement does the governor have with your organization? Is he on the board, or—"

"None."

The reporter blinked. "Uh, sorry, if I may follow up on that question, are you saying CTW has no ties to the governor at all?"

"That's correct. We're a non-governmental organization in the purest sense. As of next year, we're receiving no funding from the state at all. Politics don't come into play here, folks. We're just trying to help folks in rural communities get to work. I think that's something both sides of the party line can get behind."

Mandy marveled at his absolute cool. He hadn't even pulled that pen out of his pocket, and she wondered what had happened to it, anyway. She, on the other hand, was shaking like a leaf and was glad no one had directed a question specifically to her. Or so she thought.

When she felt a hand on her left thigh, squeezing, she looked up to find Aaron giving her an encouraging smile.

"What?" she whispered.

"You can answer."

"What was the question?"

"Mr. McNamara, can you repeat the question for my wife, please?"

She looked out into the room and found a man in rough-dried clothes with messy hair standing and squinting down at a pad. "Ms. Mc . . . uh, Mrs. Owen, I understand you developed a traffic system to coordinate the CTW staff coordinates. Is this a system that can be adapted to other businesses and organizations?"

"Possibly. Really, it started as a series of spreadsheets and my stepbrother Donald adapted it into a simple program. Each team member inputs data from their own computers and it gets compiled on our server. I make assignments based on that information."

"I'd like to learn more about it, if possible. I write for a technology magazine based out of RTP. I think a lot of small companies with remote staff would be interested in how it works."

"Of course. I can put you in touch with Donald. He loves talking geek. See me after the press conference? I'll get you his card."

Another squeeze of the thigh. This time, a *good girl* squeeze.

The questions continued for another half hour. There were a few questions about Aaron and Mandy's relationship they carefully diverted and one about Aaron's politics which he responded to with, "Politics get in the way of getting real work done, as evidenced by the last legislative session, so what exactly are you asking me?"

The reporter didn't follow up.

After that, once the crowd had seemingly determined the panel was *not*, in fact, a circus sideshow, the questions became more specific to the mission of Cars to Work—why they were there in the first place.

At the end, Aaron pulled Mandy behind the curtain the secretary had put to hide the sound equipment and gave her lips a crushing kiss.

"What was *that* for?" she panted once she'd caught her breath.

He pushed her bangs back from her eyes and kissed her again. "For being a perfect human being."

"Wow, you said it even with me wearing clothes."

He smiled that thousand-watt smile. "It's true. Think about it. I went out looking for someone to organize my staff, and ended up with a woman to run my life. It's like a buy-one, get-one special."

She laughed and gave him a swat. "I don't want to run your life, Aaron."

"Really? 'Cause from where I'm standing, it looks like you're stuck with me. Remember that whole 'better or for worse' bit? No warranties. Sold as is, sweetheart, and you've already driven me off the lot."

About the Author

Holley Trent grew up in rural eastern North Carolina. She now lives in the not-so-wild West on the Colorado Front Range, but still sounds like a Southerner.

When she's not writing or reading romance novels, she's chasing kids, yelling at incontinent cats, or trying to match mated pairs of her husband's multitude of gray socks. Like Mandy, she knows diddly-squat about cars.

Holley's an active member of RWA's Colorado Romance Writers and the CIM special interest chapter.

Find her online at *www.holleytrent.com/blog*.

In the mood for more Crimson Romance? Check out *Stuck on You* by Heather Thurmeier at CrimsonRomance.com.

.

8557424R00109

Made in the USA
San Bernardino, CA
12 February 2014